The Common Thread

By
Cubby Moreland

A Self-Published Work

P.O. Box 717
Huntingdon Valley, PA 19006

(Contributing Editor: Eric Borowsky)

Copyright © 2013 by Cubby Moreland

ISBN: 0989043002
ISBN-13: 9780989043007
Library of Congress Control # 2013903694

Acknowledgements

I would like to dedicate this book to my incredible wife Marla, my children, and their spouses, who gave me the courage to fulfill a lifelong dream. To my beautiful grandchildren, Julian, Ethan, Lila, and Pierce, you inspire me every waking minute of my life. To my brother Harry, I love you.

I would like to thank all of the people who took a sincere interest in my work, taking precious time out from their very busy schedules to read and critique this novel. They include: Dr. Paul Greenwald, Dr. Ronald Greene, Dr. Joel Garblik, Wm. Shindell, Shawn-Marie Garrett, and Joy Shindell. Cousin Tess, thank you for inspiring me to stay with it no matter how long it took. Thank you to my dear neighbor, Bill Finnel, who always listened to my thoughts. I would like to commend Carissa Marinelli for her artistic talent in designing the cover. Lastly, I want to express my gratitude to my editor Eric Borowsky, who spent many tireless hours making sure that this story is the best that it could be.

Author's Note

No one from my family of hardworking immigrants ever gave credence to or encouraged the arts as a worthwhile livelihood. It was strictly business growing up in our home. "Become a doctor, lawyer, or an accountant," my father would often say. To him, the mere thought of ever getting into the fantastical world of writing fiction was, pure and simple, hogwash. My parents didn't quite understand the aesthetic value of writing.

Once I ventured off to college, I opted to take a creative writing course to help ease the stress brought on by the rest of my rigorous course load: Statistics, Accounting, Economics and Business Law. It was a welcome change of pace and breath of fresh air, allowing me to live in an imaginary world, if only for one semester. My writing professor encouraged me to continue writing after finishing the course. "You have some raw talent. Maybe you should consider a career in writing," she suggested. I didn't follow that path at first, but I always kept her words in the back of my mind while navigating the business world and going through numerous career changes.

Inspired to revisit my long-dormant passion, I recently began work on this novel. Juggling the responsibilities of a business owner and an author, writing well into the wee hours of the morning, was a challenging, though ultimately rewarding experience. I hope you enjoy this book as much as I enjoyed writing it.

Prologue

"Hey Ed, what are you working on?" Ted asks, popping his head into my office.

"I'm still working on that Aronstein story."

"That's good. How's that coming along?" he inquires offhandedly, preoccupied with the countless thoughts constantly running through a chief editor's mind.

"It's getting there," I assure him. I have a proven track record with my boss, so he never questions my vague answers or my ability to deliver.

Just as Ted strides out of sight, Peggy, my colleague for nearly a decade, drops by my office to shoot the breeze. Peggy carefully takes a seat on the corner of my desk and crosses her legs, somehow managing to avoid disturbing all of the papers scattered on its surface. I put a pipe in my mouth; it makes me feel distinguished.

"So, how is that Aronstein case coming along, Eddie?" she pries. She must have overheard my brief conversation with Ted. "I keep hearing bits and pieces about some new revelations that have surfaced."

"It really is quite fascinating," I answer, preparing to delve into the details.

But before I can get another word out, Peggy bursts from the room to answer the phone ringing in her office. Upon her exit, I pull out the Aronstein file to review some of that new information that she mentioned.

I continually find myself drawn to this story; it plagues my mind like none other has before. Poring over the facts of this remarkable case has become second nature over the past few weeks.

Parked in front of my Smith- Corona typewriter, I soak in the panoramic view. From my partitioned office on the twenty-first floor, I can see the entire New York City skyline and a good stretch of the East River, a rare glimpse of nature for a native New Yorker. It's no wonder Peggy drops by for a chat so often.

Amidst the clanging sounds of the typewriters, ceaseless ringing of phones, and shuffling of papers in our busy office, I often take solace in the picturesque scenery. It's about as picturesque as it gets around here.

My walls aren't nearly as glamorous. They're plastered with some of my best work. Rapes, murders, robberies, abductions—I've covered them all at my longtime post on the crime beat. Despite their graphic nature, I'll proudly share the gruesome details with anyone who stops in to sneak a glance out my window. It's pretty disturbing stuff.

My desk is cluttered with the usual mountain of notes, but a picture of my beautiful family rises above the mess. I'll often drift back and forth between my glorious view of the world and that photograph. It really makes me appreciate what life is all about; certainly not rapes and murders.

More scattered files cover my floor, and some even lean up against the wall. Although they are strewn about in total disarray, those folders contain all of the vital information I've collected as an investigative reporter.

I switch on my little electric coffee pot, which hums away as it brews that magical brown stuff that gives me the energy to get through each day. From time to time, I'll drown out the whirring noise with the sounds of the Beatles and the Beach Boys, which blare from my small radio. Good oldies music is the perfect complement to a strong cup of joe and the spectacular view.

I arrive each morning articulately dressed, but at this point in the day, my jacket is draped over my chair, my sleeves are rolled up, and my tie is loosely hanging from my collar.

This job is stressful, with the onslaught of looming deadlines, but every so often it provides moments of enlightenment. I've begun to reexamine my own life, my true worth to society, since returning to the Aronstein case. The immense pain that Aronstein must have endured in jail all these years, separated from his family, would bring any man to his breaking point, even a convicted murderer like him.

With only a few hours to get this story to press, I insert the blank sheet of paper in my typewriter and crank the roll bar with both of my hands. I begin to type, immersing myself in the sensational Aronstein story one last time.

Chapter 1

A blackened cloud hovered over cell # 132E at Auburn Correctional Facility. It was the eve of Michael Aronstein's execution, a cold and blistery night in February of 1975. At the young age of 42, he was to be put to death for brutally murdering his lover.

His appeals had all been denied. Michael had no choice but to accept his fate. While languishing on death row for eight long years, he'd become accustomed to loneliness.

His last request was a visit from Andrew Fox, his best friend and defense attorney, and Rabbi Meyer Sakowitz, the Aronstein family's spiritual guide for as long as Michael could remember. Both men had played integral roles in Michael's life, and now, more than ever, he desperately needed their comfort. The previous day's emotional farewell to his immediate family had been devastating.

The guards unlocked the cell door and swung it open with a loud clang. Andrew and Rabbi Sakowitz entered his cell, arms outstretched. They had come to pay their final respects to their dear friend.

Not Michael Aronstein, the cold-blooded killer, but Michael Aronstein, the blonde-haired, wide-eyed friend that they remembered fondly. Cherishing what would be his last human contact, Michael smiled for the first time in many months. Vivid

1

memories rushed to the forefront of his mind, and he felt a semblance of peacefulness.

Michael sat down on his cot beside the rabbi. Andrew took a spot on the floor and leaned against the wall of the tiny cell.

"How are you, Michael?" asked the rabbi, as he placed his hand on Michael's shoulder.

"Not so good." He shook his head from side to side discontentedly.

"I understand. Few of us could withstand this pain."

"Life's just not fair," Michael cried out, wiping tears away with his right shirt- sleeve, "Why me? Why did this happen to—"

"You're going to a better place," Andrew interjected. "We'll all meet up there together someday."

Michael solemnly nodded. He'd become well-versed in the multitude of theories on the Afterlife since his incarceration.

Rabbi Sakowitz resumed his consolatory speech, reassuring Michael of his status as one of God's children. Michael listened intently, absorbing the words of the man whose advice he had always sought in times of need.

Sakowitz stared directly into his eyes and uttered, "None of us can control our destiny, Michael. We can only make the best of what God has set before us. Today you must be thankful for what He gave you, not angry for what He took away."

Michael took that last bit to heart.

"Just think about how blessed you were to have such wonderful parents. I can still picture their beaming faces on the day of your bris. They raised you to be such a wonderful young man. Just think of your Bar Mitzvah day and how proud they were of your accomplishments."

Michael recalled looking out at the congregation that day and envisioned the goofy smiles plastered on his parents' faces. He couldn't help but grin himself.

"The Lord gave you a beautiful wife and children," the rabbi continued. "I was honored to attend your wedding and bless your girls when they were newborns."

Those were good times, Michael thought. Back when he could envision only better times ahead.

"You experienced many joys throughout your life. The material things you had were only borrowed. You can't take them with you. We all have to surrender them sooner or later. In the end, all we can hold onto are the happy memories."

"I'm so grateful," Andrew added, "to have a friend like you. Nothing can erase all those good times we had growing up. You were the brother I never had, buddy."

Touched, Michael felt the tears well up in his eyes. But as the evening continued, they turned into laughter, and frowns turned into smiles. They reminisced some more about the good old days—from kindergarten to proms and everything in between.

"Andrew, can you promise me that you'll take care of my family?" Michael requested. "The kids, they'll need you."

"Of course, Mike."

"And one last thing—can you give them this letter? One last message from their father."

Andrew nodded and embraced his friend. Michael turned to his rabbi.

"My last wish is for you to bless me as you did on the day of my bris." Rabbi Sakowitz stood, lifted one arm over his head, and blessed Michael with a traditional Jewish prayer.

The time for the visitors' departure rapidly approached. Andrew and Rabbi Sakowitz bade farewell to Michael one last time and shuffled out of the cell. That was it. It was the last time he'd ever see Andrew, his trusted companion. Both men held back their emotions until they had separated, after which they broke down in tears.

The following night, two armed prison guards, Warden McCluskey, and Rabbi Sakowitz arrived at Michael's cell to escort him to the death chambers. Michael took one last look at the few personal effects he had accumulated during his time at Auburn. He left behind some photographs of his family, a portable cassette player, a transistor radio, three paperback novels, a copy of the Holy Script, and his diary. He hoped they would find their way to his family.

"Are you ready to go?" asked Warden McCluskey.

With his head bowed, Michael silently nodded. This final journey down the hallway would end at the electric chair. Handcuffed and shackled, Michael slowly entered the room to find another prison guard, a doctor, and Rabbi Sakowitz waiting to send him on his way. Aside from his ashy complexion, Michael exhibited few other signs of apprehension. This was his fate; there was no turning back.

The electric chair sat in the center of the room. Michael tried to focus his attention elsewhere, but couldn't look away from his final resting place. He couldn't see the various state officials, media, and other witnesses seated behind the room's mirrored glass, nor could he hear the roar of the protesters outside.

"This is Murder, Kill the Switch," they chanted, their cardboard signs slicing through the brisk air. A hearse sat by a nearby loading dock, patiently waiting for its passenger.

The guards removed Michael's shackles and replaced his handcuffs with leather straps, which they tightly secured around his wrists. Bewildered, Michael stared up at the ceiling, wondering about his soul's next destination.

Rabbi Sakowitz removed the prayer cap from Michael's head. The doctor applied tape to his eyes to prevent them from popping out of their sockets when the electrical jolt surged through his body.

Michael's lower lip quivered uncontrollably, and his heart pulsated. A cold sweat soaked the palms of his hands as his pores opened up like the gates to a dam.

With less than a minute of his life remaining, Michael uttered, "God be with me, He knows that I didn't do this."

His eyes closed, he began reflecting back on his life.

Chapter 2

World War II concluded in September of 1945, and countless American soldiers came home victorious, though not without battle scars. Families reunited with their loved ones, and signs of hope and optimism were in the air.

Twelve year-old Michael Aronstein prepared for his Bar Mitzvah ceremony, the start of his transition into manhood. His parents, Sadie and Herbie, anticipated the occasion even more fervently than he did.

After all the complications they encountered a decade earlier while attempting to conceive, the Aronsteins felt blessed to have guided their son to this important moment in his life. And in four more years, they would do the same for their daughter, Rebecca.

The family resided in the vibrant borough of Brooklyn, and, when he wasn't forced to study, Michael spent much of his time playing games in the streets with his large circle of friends. They all had met back in kindergarten, when the most important things in their lives were perfecting the finger paintings they took home to their mothers. Michael enjoyed every waking minute with his buddies, whether it was spent playing a game of wall ball, stickball, or just gossiping about the cute girls in their class.

The entire gang came from hardworking, lower middle class families, though their ethnicities varied from Italian to Irish to Eastern European. What they all had in common was the competitive drive to prevail in the day's athletic event.

One crisp fall evening, they were in the middle of an intense game of stickball. The score was tied, and the sun had just started to set. The daylight waning, Michael stepped up to the plate for what was sure to be his last at-bat of the game.

"Come on Aronstein, smack the hell out of it," shouted Andrew. Michael just smirked and pushed his curly blonde locks to the side as he took his stance.

"Here comes the curve," Alan warned, as he released the half pimple ball with a twist of his hand. Michael dropped his shoulder and took a big swing of the sawed-off broomstick, missing by a hair.

"Big whiffer!" Nick cried with glee. His shiny, pitch-black pompadour marked him as the only Italian of the group. He also retained bits of his parents' colorful accents.

"Strike one!" Freddie yelled.

"Ah he's a wimp," Nick chortled, as Alan released the ball for a second time.

Again, Michael's swing was off target. Before his body twisted back into its original position, Sadie, his mother, called out to him from a third-floor window above.

"Michael! It's time to come in!"

"I'll be in soon. Right after this game," he insisted.

"Don't you have homework to do?"

"I do, but it won't take too long."

"How about your Bar Mitzvah studies?" she reminded him.

"Mom, can it wait for just one more minute? The game's tied."

"I've heard that one before. Please come up now. It's getting dark already."

7

Michael dropped the makeshift bat and submitted to her request. He knew his parents well enough; they would often vocalize their high expectations for his Bar Mitzvah ceremony. He had never let them down before.

Michael ran through the front door of the apartment building, his hair flapping in the wind. He bounded up the stairs and burst through the door of his apartment.

"Don't you have homework to do?" his mother asked once again. "Not to mention your Bar Mitzvah prayers. It's coming up rather soon; practically right around the corner."

"I know, I know. I heard you the first time."

"Well, it doesn't look like you heard me. Get to work!"

"Mom, I just got home from school. Just give me some time to relax and have a snack!" he snapped. Michael's face reddened to the shade of an apple as blood rushed to his forehead.

"Okay," she relented. Content with getting his way, Michael softened as well.

"I promise I'll get to it soon," he assured her. "I'll do some schoolwork first, and then I'll study my Torah portion."

As his mother prepared dinner for the family, Michael finished his snacks and holed up in his bedroom to complete his schoolwork. He spent an hour on homework and then practiced for his Bar Mitzvah service.

He placed a record on his RCA Victor phonograph, opened up his book, and chanted each prayer along with the recording until he had it completely memorized. Becky and her friend Rochelle could hear his chanting through the walls.

"Mom, can you tell him to stop singing so loud? We can't concentrate!"

"Concentrate on what? Your dollhouse?" Michael screamed back.

"Michael, sing softer!" Sadie commanded.

"Fine!"

The doorbell rang, and Sadie raised the window and stuck out her head.

"It's Miriam," a voice shouted. "I need a gown mended. Can I come up?"

"Yes, of course," Sadie replied.

A loyal customer for many years, Miriam had also referred many other women in need of a seamstress to Sadie throughout the years. She was the type of patron who didn't hesitate to walk right in the front door without so much as a knock.

"How are you, Miriam?" Sadie greeted her.

"I'm doing well. How about you?"

"Busy, busy, busy! Thank God! What can I do for you today?"

"I need this dress hemmed for my nephew's wedding next month," said Miriam.

Sadie held it up and took a look.

"That is a beautiful gown. Where is the affair being held?"

"Up in the mountains at the Concord Resort. It's a whole weekend-long extravaganza."

"I'm sure you'll have a wonderful time," Sadie said. "Our family vacations there every summer. The food is delicious and they stuff you to the gills. You can eat whatever you want and as much as you like."

"I've already heard all about it from some of my other friends," Miriam said. "They raved about it, too. We're all very excited."

"You better go on a diet to prepare," Sadie kidded. "Because after a couple of days at Concord, you'll be back here asking me to let out your clothes again."

Sadie held some pins between her lips as Miriam entered the bathroom to change into the gown. Miriam returned to the mirrored corner of the room that served as Sadie's workspace and scrutinized herself in the mirror.

Sadie told her how gorgeous she looked in the dress, noting how nicely it shaped her body, and finished pinning the waist. She bid Miriam adieu, reminding her to return next week to pick it up.

Dinnertime came shortly after Sadie finished with her customer. Her husband Herbie arrived home from the butcher shop, where he toiled day in and day out, and the family gathered around the kitchen table to eat.

"So how are my children doing today?" Herbie asked. "How are those Bar Mitzvah lessons coming along, son?"

"It's a work in progress," Michael admitted. "I've been trying to sing it just like Rabbi Sakowitz does on the record, but I still stumble in some spots."

"Try to learn as quickly as you can," Sadie interjected.

"I know, Mom. You've told me a million times: It's right around the corner."

"Sometime this week, both of you need to be fitted for new suits. Becky, you'll need a fancy dress for the services and luncheon," Sadie continued.

"I'll just find something in my closet. We don't have to spend the money," Herbie insisted.

"Over my dead body will you wear an old raggedy suit," she exclaimed. "You'll come to Macy's with me to pick out something nice for your son's Bar Mitzvah."

Without taking a breath, she added, "Herbie, do you know where father's tallis is? He'll need to wear it up on the bimah."

"The one from his bris? How could I forget? It's sitting in the closet."

He turned his attention to Becky. "Before you know it, it will be your Bat Mitzvah and we'll be having the same discussion."

"I know, Daddy," she said, clutching his arm.

Chapter 3

*M*ichael truly enjoyed his life as a seventh grader. He excelled in the classroom, receiving all A's on his report card, and out in the schoolyard, fraternizing with his large group of friends. On the weekends, they hung out at the movies or the bowling alley that stayed open late. Michael was always immaculately dressed in the latest fashions. He was one of the most popular guys in his class, and all of the girls swarmed around him.

Michael embraced his impending manhood by learning as much as he could about more adult subjects. One seemingly average Wednesday, his buddy Nick invited all the guys to his house to unveil the interesting discovery he'd made in his parents' closet. It was a perfect afternoon for such an occasion, as both of Nick's parents were at work. Given only the slightest hint at what Nick had unearthed, Alan, Freddie, Andrew, and Michael awaited the presentation with a mixture of excitement and anxiety.

After dramatically descending the stairs, Nick dropped an unmarked cardboard box on the kitchen table. All the boys jumped up to get a peek inside. Nestled atop a pile of old magazines was an old film reel labeled only with an "XXX," the most precious series of letters in the English language. At this age, their hormones were just beginning to kick in, and none of them had ever experienced or witnessed any sexual acts. All they knew was what they had heard from the older kids in the neighborhood.

Nick ushered them into the basement and set up the projector. He fed the reel-to-reel tape through the camera's lens and pointed the projector at a blank wall. The boys settled into comfortable positions on the floor as Nick turned off the lights off and pulled down the shades.

The movie began to flicker, and the room suddenly went silent as they all focused on the screen. Michael was particularly captivated by the very adult images; he felt a sense of arousal sweep through his body.

The following Saturday evening, he and Andrew congregated with friends in a female classmate's basement. They listened to records on a phonograph and munched on snacks until one girl suggested that they play a game of spin the bottle.

The kids sat down on the floor and arranged themselves in a circle. Michael had his sights set on some of the girls, many of whom had their hearts set on kissing him, as well.

The game started, and Babs, one of the overweight and unattractive girls at the party, gave the bottle a twirl with all of her might. It slowed to a halt and pointed directly at Michael. She was ecstatic, but Michael made little effort to conceal his disappointment.

Babs grabbed his hand and pulled him into the closet. Raucous laughter erupted.

In the darkness of the closet, Babs clutched the door handle tightly to prevent Michael from escaping. She slobbered him with wet kisses for a few moments and then relented. Making the best of the situation, Michael responded by groping every part of her body. Informal as it was, this was his first anatomy lesson.

Once the hasty make out session concluded, Michael exited and embarrassingly wiped his mouth with his forearm. Babs emerged, looking radiant as ever. The news of their encounter spread around the school like wildfire, but Michael managed to take the gentle ribbing he received in stride. He was already starting to feel like more of a man.

Michael outgrew those Junior High parties by the time he matriculated onto high school, where he discovered a whole new social world. He encountered new faces, a new educational atmosphere, and more challenging courses. There was greater emphasis placed upon learning, rather than discipline, in this new environment. The strong educational values instilled in him by his parents motivated him to gain acceptance to a respectable college.

Through the tenth and eleventh grades, Michael excelled in his studies and became a mainstay on the honor roll. He worked hard to become the star pitcher of the baseball team and even practiced in the high school gym during the winter months. Michael's popularity, good looks, and academic achievements helped propel him to the spotlight of his class. His circle of friends cherished his honesty, sincerity, and integrity. Plus, he could woo any girl with his charisma.

Michael entered the twelfth grade in September of 1950. On the first day of classes, as usual, the students reported to their homerooms to receive their rosters and new locker assignments. More than just an administrative necessity, the gathering was an opportunity to get acquainted with any new students in the class. After roll call and some other announcements, the school bell rang, alerting students to move on to their next class.

Michael removed a key from his pocket and inserted it into the lock dangling from the door. As he shuffled through his belongings, he heard the metallic echo of a nearby locker. He turned to his right to find a cute blonde-haired, blue-eyed girl fiddling with her keys.

Michael thought that he already knew all of the pretty girls in school, but this beauty had certainly never crossed his path. She must be a new student, he thought to himself. Michael waved hello, and she looked up from her crouched position, acknowledging him with a radiant smile and reciprocal wave of her hand.

"Hi, I'm Michael," he said.

"Lauren. Lauren Peterson," she replied.

"Nice to meet you, Lauren" he said, extending his hand for a friendly shake. Obliged, she rose to a standing position and shook it.

"I haven't seen you in school before. Are you new?" Michael asked.

"Yes, today's my first day. My family just moved into town over the summer."

"What grade are you in?"

"Eleventh."

"Well, good luck with the transition. If you need help with anything, anytime, don't hesitate to ask. I've lived here all my life, so I know every nook and cranny of the borough," he touted.

"Thank you," she cordially replied.

"See you around," he avowed. He gathered his books and headed for his next class.

"Hey Mike! Come here," a voice beckoned. Michael spotted Andrew waving him down to the other side of the hallway.

"I want to ask you something." The tall, handsome, and well-built quarterback of the football team, Andrew was popular in his own right. He attracted nearly as many girls as Michael did.

15

"Did you check your roster yet?" Andrew asked.

"Yeah, I wonder if we have any classes together?"

They both took out their schedules to compare. They were ecstatic to find that they would share two classes and a lunch period that semester.

"See you at lunch," Michael said as he hurried off to his next class.

Lunch period arrived, and an array of students ranging from grades ten through twelve amassed in the cafeteria. Michael and Andrew sat down at their usual table and opened their brown-bagged lunches. The other guys who rounded out their circle of friends, Alan, Freddie and Nick, joined them.

"What's up guys?" Michael bellowed.

"Shit, I got some tough courses this term," Nick cried. "If I don't get my act together, I'll be headed to summer school instead of college like you two Einsteins," he told Michael and Andrew.

"If you'd stop laying all the girls and spend a little less time tinkering with that old jalopy you drive, maybe you'll make it down the aisle with us," Andrew said, provoking raucous laughter.

"Did anybody see that new chick with the blonde hair, blue eyes, and ponytail down to her ass?" asked Alan.

"Oh, I did. Her locker's right next to mine," Michael bragged.

"Well aren't you the lucky one?" sneered Freddie.

"Speaking of the devil, look who's over there." Andrew pointed at Lauren, who was searching for a table with a tray in her hands.

"Wow, she really is drop dead gorgeous," Freddie exclaimed.

Nick let out a soft whistle and declared, "Can't wait to ask that babe out."

"Not so fast," Michael corrected him. "Didn't we just talk about you keeping your hands off the girls?"

"Yeah, but those were just jokes, right?" Nick asked.

"Honestly, I was already planning on taking her out myself. I think I'd do a good job of showing her around town, if you know what I mean." Michael joked.

"Why don't you start slow?" Andrew suggested. "I'm taking Tammy to the drive-in this Saturday. Come with us."

"I don't know anything about her. She could already have a boyfriend for all I know."

"Well if you don't ask her, you'll never find out," Andrew added.

"Alright. But only when the time is right," Michael said.

For the rest of the school day, Michael searched for an opportunity to catch up with Lauren and extend the invite. Unfortunately, she had left school early.

But that didn't stop him from thinking about her. In fact, he thought about her all night long. He rehearsed his proposition over and over again, as if it were his Bar Mitzvah portion. It had to be flawless, for she was much too beautiful to accept anything less.

The following morning, Michael patiently waited for Lauren at his locker. Crowds of students passed through the corridors, but she was nowhere to be found.

Disappointed, Michael moved on to Chemistry class, where he met up with Andrew.

"What'd she say?"

"Nothing yet. I haven't even seen her since lunch yesterday."

"Come on! Get your ass in gear. You can make it happen," Andrew declared. "Besides, I already told Tammy all about her. She's excited to meet this goddess. Don't let us down."

"I won't," Michael responded with confidence.

After Chemistry, Andrew and Michael parted ways. Michael ran back to his locker to retrieve his packed lunch and dispose of some books. He lingered there with hopes of running into Lauren. He scanned the hallway, attempting to look casual; he wanted their meeting to appear coincidental.

After several minutes, Lauren appeared, turning the corner and heading for her locker. Michael quickly looked away and pretended to shuffle through his belongings. When she reached her locker, Michael made his move.

"Hi Lauren. How's it going?"

"Not bad."

"So. I was wondering. Do you have plans this Saturday night?"

"That depends. What do you have in mind?"

"My friend Andrew and his girlfriend are seeing a movie at the drive-in, and I'd like you to come along as my date."

"That would be great," she gushed, her smile glowing.

"Great!" said Michael. "That's just great!" He returned a matching grin, but just stood there silently. He had only rehearsed up to that point.

"Do you want my phone number or something?" Michael nodded, and she pulled out a piece of paper and pen.

"Where are you headed now?" Michael inquired.

"To the cafeteria."

"Me too. How about I carry your books over there?"

"By all means," she assented. She dropped her heavy stack of books into his arms, and they set off towards the lunchroom, making small talk.

Upon reaching the cafeteria, they separated and sat down at their respective tables.

"See you later, Lauren." Michael said, waving his hand. "Don't forget to call me with the details," she replied. "I won't." "Great!" She did her best to replicate his goofy grin.

Chapter 4

*A*ndrew elected to drive to the movies that Saturday night. He arrived at Michael's house with Tammy in the front seat. From there, they drove to Lauren's house, a two-story brownstone in Brooklyn Heights. Michael got out of the vehicle and rang the doorbell.

Lauren's mother greeted him at the door. Mrs. Peterson bore a strong resemblance to her daughter; it was in her eyes. Her face was made up just so—enough to accentuate her features, but not overly caked on.

"Hi Mrs. Peterson, I'm Michael Aronstein," he said. He shook her hand and took a step inside.

"It's a pleasure to meet you. Call me Martha. I insist."

The slightly older, gruff man sitting in the living room set down his newspaper and rose from his chair. He gave Michael a firm handshake.

"Hello. I'm Victor, Lauren's father," he boomed.

"Nice to meet you, sir."

"Come on in, Michael. Lauren has been expecting you," Mrs. Peterson said. "Lauren! There's a young gentleman here to see you," she called out.

"I'll be right there," Lauren shouted from upstairs.

"Sit down. Make yourself comfortable," Martha instructed.

Just as Michael touched down on the couch cushion, Lauren made her way down the long staircase to the foyer. Michael waited there, becoming more and more awestruck at her beauty with each step she took.

"Hi Michael!" she said with a smile, jarring him out of his temporary stupor.

As they walked out the front door, Mrs. Peterson called out, "Have a great time. Don't get home too late!"

Tammy opened the passenger door of Andrew's two-door Chrysler coupe, and Lauren and Michael jumped into the backseat. After a quick introduction, Andrew sped off for the Skyline Drive-in Theater in Lyndhurst. It was over by the south shore, off Sunset Boulevard.

Upon arriving at the theater, Michael and Andrew left the car to get popcorn and beverages from the concession stand. They returned to find Tammy and Lauren deep in conversation. They had gotten quite acquainted during their absence.

"Then my dad accepted the promotion, and we left Minnesota to come here," Lauren explained. "Well, we're all happy to have you." Tammy gave her a reassuring pat on the arm.

The feature film, *All the King's Men*, was projected onto a giant screen in front of all the cars. Lauren, Tammy, Michael, and Andrew munched on popcorn and slurped their sodas as they soaked in the drama of Willie Stark's rise to power. Lauren looked around at windows of the vehicles parked beside them and spied some couples kissing. Some cars showed had no visible signs of passengers, indicating that its passengers had lied down on the car seat to get intimate.

Before they knew it, Tammy and Andrew started kissing in the front seat. This was Michael's chance. He turned towards

Lauren and gazed into her eyes. She looked through him with her piercing blue eyes.

Lauren let loose a nervous chuckle. The ice was broken, and they shared a passionate kiss. A warm feeling permeated through Michael's body. He could sense she felt the same sensation.

After the credits rolled, they decided to get a bite to eat at a local diner before heading home. Michael, feeling more comfortable with Lauren, alternated between holding her hand and putting his arm around her shoulders as they sat in the booth.

Lauren fit in quite well with Michael's friends. She was pleasant, outgoing, and seemed genuine. Her intelligence was up to par, and she conversed with them on a comfortable level. Michael didn't view the date as some sort of a personality test, but he was mindful of his friends' approval. He had dated some other girls who just didn't fit the mold. He wanted to avoid that path, if possible.

"She's quite a girl," Andrew remarked after the girls stepped away to the bathroom. "She seems to get along really well with Tammy, unlike some of your other bimbos."

"She is different." Michael smirked. "I've never felt this great about a first date."

"Well, that's a good sign," Andrew said.

"I hope she likes me. I'd love to take her out again."

Lauren and Tammy returned to the booth, their makeup freshened and clothes tidied. After the meal, they drove back to Lauren's house in Brooklyn Heights, and Michael exited to walk her to the front door.

"I had a great time, Michael."

"I did too."

He put his arms around her and shared another kiss. As their lips parted, Michael uttered, "I'll call you later."

"Don't forget," Lauren cooed.

He walked towards the awaiting car, but turned back to make sure that she had gotten inside safely. She looked just as beautiful when she walked away.

Chapter 5

Spring had truly sprung in Brooklyn. Michael awoke, exhilarated, to a brightly shining sun and light blue skies, on the Saturday morning of his prom. He spent the morning picking up his tuxedo and a bouquet of flowers. He also got his hair trimmed for good measure.

Lauren's day didn't go nearly as smoothly. She dashed through the city to pick up her gown, which needed last-minute alterations. After stopping at the beauty parlor, she had to swing by the flower shop to pick up a boutonniere for Michael.

She finally got it all together and started getting dressed, making sure to stuff her bra with a tiny bit of toilet tissue to enlarge her breasts a barely perceptible amount.

"Mom, can you come up here for a minute? I need your help," she shouted, as she herself in front of the mirror. Her mother bounded into her room in a flash.

"Oh my God! You look like Cinderella, like a breath of fresh air. Wait! Let me fix your dress for a second." She gave it a tug at the waist while Lauren cupped her breasts with both hands.

Michael, dressed in his black tailored tuxedo, arrived at Lauren's house with a bouquet of flowers at his side. Some close family friends and neighbors greeted him at the door and complimented his ensemble.

Michael responded to their kind words with some of his own, until the focus abruptly, and rightfully so, shifted from him. Lauren had come to the top of the steps, looking beautiful as ever in her long, shimmering pink satin gown. She wore her hair up, with a single curl hanging down each side of her face, and accessorized with some of her mother's jewelry. She lit up the room with her sheer elegance. Michael offered her the flowers, and Lauren pinned a white boutonniere on his lapel.

The crowd beamed as brightly as their cameras' flashes. After the photo session, everyone extended their good wishes, and Michael ushered Lauren back to his home to introduce her to his family for the first time.

The Aronsteins were beyond excited. Upon their entrance, each family member greeted Michael and Lauren with a warm embrace and kiss on the cheek. They welcomed Lauren into their home with open arms.

With delight, Sadie told Lauren, "You look so beautiful, like a movie star. Your dress is gorgeous. I wish I had your shape," she kidded.

Lauren smiled and accepted the barrage of compliments with gratitude.

"My son sure has good taste," Sadie added. Becky took some snapshots with her Kodak flash camera, and, soon after, everyone exchanged cordial farewells. Michael and Lauren set off for the pre-prom party at Tammy's house.

Tammy's family served hors d'oeuvres and non-alcoholic cocktails to their guests. Alan, Freddie, and Nick, and their dates filled out rest of the bunch. All of the girls were cordial towards Lauren, but she could detect hints of jealousy behind their greetings.

Everyone indulged in the pigs in a blanket, cocktail shrimp, and stuffed miniature crab cakes. Nibbling at the petite food, they exchanged compliments.

In another corner of the room, Nick and Freddie commiserated while their dates were in the bathroom.

"That Lauren is a knockout," Freddie said.

"Boy, would I like to stick my sausage into her," Nick joked, holding up a cocktail weenie. "But don't tell Michael, or--" He violently gnashed into the hot dog, leaving Freddie in stitches.

The party wound down, and everyone excitedly hopped into their cars to head for the Drake Hotel in downtown Manhattan. They entered the hotel lobby and spotted a crowd gathered around the elevator. They all piled in and rode it up one floor to the ballroom level. Teachers and chaperones, seated at fold-up tables, accepted the students' tickets and presented them with the assigned seating arrangements.

Michael and his sizeable crew entered the ballroom, where the sounds of a big band electrified the air. Streamers hung from the chandeliers, and flowers sat on linen tablecloths, accompanied by nice silverware and china. Students danced to the beat of the drums, and the brass section blasted its horns.

The boys' formal black tuxedos provided a contrast to the rainbow of shaped gowns that dotted the ballroom floor. Michael and Lauren couldn't wait to get on the dance floor. They didn't even sit down; they launched right into the jitterbug.

After a few more tunes, Michael and Lauren, considerably winded, sat down to eat their dinner entrees—chicken breast with mashed potatoes and string beans. Alan, who sat on the prom committee, made sure that the whole group was assigned to the same table.

"The school did a great job," Lauren said.

"I don't mean to brag, but I was on the planning committee," touted Alan.

"This calls for a toast to Alan's fabulous planning," Andrew suggested.

They all raised their glasses and clinked them together.

"So what do you plan to do after graduation?" Tammy asked Nick, who was taking another gulp of the sparkling cider.

"I'm joining the Army," he replied, his smile gleaming. "Just like my Pop."

"My dad fought over in Europe during World War II, too. He was just happy to come home in one piece," Freddie added.

"Mine was in the Navy. He sailed on a battleship in the Pacific fleet. You should hear his stories about all of the Japanese planes they shot down," boasted Alan.

"Sorry to change the subject," Tammy apologized, "But I love your jewelry, Lauren. Where did you get it?"

"I borrowed it from my mom."

"She has great taste," Michael said, winking at Lauren.

The night passed rather quickly. It was soon time for the band to take a break to announce the Prom King and Queen. A drum roll sounded, and everyone focused on the bandleader, who held the telltale index card in his hand. The ballroom was dead silent; everyone anxiously awaited the crowning of this year's winners.

"Boys and girls, let's hear a round of applause for your Prom Queen...Lauren Peterson!" The crowd erupted in applause and whistles as Lauren, flabbergasted, rushed to the center stage. The bandleader placed the crown upon her head and handed her a bouquet of red roses. Another drum roll sounded, and the bandleader continued, "And please welcome to the stage, your Prom King.... Michael Aronstein!" To raucous applause, Michael hopped up on the stage to embrace his Queen. Their faces beamed as they descended to the floor to share their inaugural dance.

The evening concluded, and couples exchanged warm goodbyes as they trickled out of the ballroom. Intending to party the night away, Michael and Andrew had reserved a suite at the Drake for their entire table. They extended the celebration up in their room, enjoying refreshments that were spiked with the alcohol that Nick had smuggled in. As they imbibed more and more, the silly behavior and laughter began.

"Did you see that fat chick in the red dress? Her boobs were hanging out all over the dance floor," Nick chuckled.

"Yeah, and she was wrapped around her date like a snake choking its prey," Alan added.

"That's disgusting," snapped Tammy.

"How about that jerk who was dancing all sloppily, bumping into everybody. He thought he owned the dance floor," Andrew said.

"I was ready to punch him out," Freddie declared.

"Let's raise our glass to Alan one more time," Andrew suggested, as he poured scotch into everyone's glasses.

Everyone became much more intoxicated as the night progressed into the wee hours. "I have a great idea!" slurred Tammy. She went over to the phonograph and put on some slow, romantic music. Andrew dimmed the lights to set the mood. Everyone took their partners' hands and slow-danced to the ballad. Michael pulled Lauren close to him and kissed her lips, neck, and ears.

As the song wound down, he guided her into a bedroom as a captain navigates his ship. He shut the door and maneuvered Lauren into bed. Kissing her passionately, Michael gently removed one article of her clothing at a time until she was stark naked. She pulled Michael towards her, unloosening his belt, giving him the green light. She wanted to feel every inch of him. Michael responded in kind and thrusted, whispering, "I love you, Prom Queen" in her ear. "I love you too, Michael," she said.

Losing her virginity transformed Lauren from a teen to a woman. Her and Michael's relationship had reached a new plateau on that special evening.

Chapter 6

7he prom weekend cemented Michael and Lauren's relationship. Michael graduated from high school and spent nearly the entire summer at Lauren's side. Michael's family invited her on their annual vacation to the Catskills, and the Petersons reciprocated with an invitation to sail the seas of Cape Cod. On the drive home, Victor stopped by Boston University so that Michael could take a look at the campus where he'd be spending the next four years. He and Lauren strolled through the center of town, making note of all the nice restaurants at which they hoped to dine together. There was no question that they would stay together while Michael attended college.

That summer soon turned to fall, and the leaves on the treetops took on various shades of gold and brown. Michael's friends prepared to go their separate ways. Andrew enrolled in Columbia University, Nick joined the Army, Alan landed a job as a bookkeeper for a manufacturer in downtown Manhattan, and Freddie started work as a salesman in a local men's shoe store. Lauren and Tammy entered their senior year of high school.

It was time for Michael to spread his wings and venture off to BU. He spent the entire day before his departure with Lauren, savoring every precious minute before he left her behind. They shopped for everything Michael could have possibly needed at school, including a decorative picture frame to place on his nightstand. Lauren pulled their prom picture out of her handbag and held it up to the frame. It looked perfect.

After helping Michael pack for his journey, Lauren took him to one of their favorite spots, the banks of the Passaic River. They watched the crew team practice and enjoyed the tranquil sounds of nature one last time. They sat side by side, gazing at the swift-flowing waters as they said their last goodbyes.

"I'm going to miss you so much, Michael," Lauren said. "Things won't be the same without you."

"I'll miss you too," he replied, tightly clutching her hand.

"Promise me that you won't date any other girls," she insisted.

"I promise, but only if you don't find yourself another fella." Lauren playfully slapped him on the hand.

"I don't know how I'll make it through this last year of school without all you guys. Now it's just Tammy and me."

She rested her head on Michael's shoulder and nestled up under his neck.

"Thanksgiving, Christmas, and spring break are just around the corner," he assured her. "We'll see each other then."

"That's not soon enough," she shot back.

"It's just a few months."

"I guess you're right—but can you promise me one more thing?"

"Of course—as long as you promise this is the last one you'll ask for."

"Tell me right now that you'll be here for my senior prom."

"There's no way I'd miss it," he said.

They kissed and squeezed each other with all their might. A little girl passed by and shouted, "Look, Mommy! They're in love!"

Michael and Lauren couldn't help but smile.

Chapter 7

7he day after Labor Day, Michael set off for college. Accompanied by his parents, he found his dorm room and started to unpack his belongings. It was a chaotic scene; families bustled through the halls of the dorm.

Michael's roommate soon arrived. He seemed just as anxious to get situated.

"Hi, I'm Dennis, and these are my parents, Sylvia and Jack." They all carried suitcases at their sides.

"I'm Michael. It's nice to meet you. These are my folks, Sadie and Herb. So where are you from?"

"Philadelphia," Dennis responded. "How about yourself?"

"I'm from Brooklyn, New York."

The families engaged in small talk as the boys stuffed their drawers with clothes, made the beds, and decorated the room.

Once the room was suitably arranged to Sadie's taste, Michael asked Dennis and his parents to join them for lunch. The invitation was declined, so the Aronsteins set off to tour the campus and familiarize themselves with the university's facilities. Michael's parents were very proud of his accomplishments and honored that he was able to attend such a fine university, which was home to such a diverse array of students.

Having worked up an appetite, Michael and his family stopped at Suzy's, a diner that advertised the "Best Lobster Roll on Campus". After a short wait, they were seated in a cozy booth in the corner.

"Aren't you going to miss us?" Sadie asked, as she reached for a menu.

"I will, but I have to grow up sometime."

"Not too fast, now. Don't get yourself into any trouble," his father warned.

"What do you mean by that, Dad?"

"I mean wild parties with girls and stuff."

"Don't come home with any babies, now," his mother kidded. "Not until you and Lauren make it official." They broke into laughter.

"What courses are you taking this semester?" she asked.

"I have to fulfill some liberal arts requirements before I can declare my major."

"Have you thought any more about what you'd like to study? Or what you'd like to do in the future?" his father asked.

"I think I'd like to do something on Wall Street. Finance, that sort of thing."

"That's interesting," Herb remarked.

"Why don't you become a doctor?" his mother interjected. "You'd make a wonderful living." Michael just rolled his eyes.

"Speaking of Lauren—are you still going to date? How often will you see her?" Sadie pried.

"She's already planned a visit for a weekend next month. I'll write to her, call her on the phone. We'll make it work."

When the time to say goodbye finally arrived, Michael hugged his parents and wished them well on the long journey back to Brooklyn. As Sadie lingered on Michael's image in the rearview mirror, tears came to her eyes. This was the first time her son would be away from home for more than a few days.

"It feels like just yesterday that we celebrated his first birthday," she said to her husband.

"And when he became a Bar Mitzvah," Herbie added, as he gave his wife a consoling pat on the thigh.

"I'm going to miss him," she cried, wiping the tears away with a handkerchief.

Without anyone to answer to, Michael fully embraced his independence. He spent the first few days buying his books and locating all of the lecture halls where his classes would be held.

The educational requirements for college were far different from what Michael was accustomed to. Attendance wasn't mandatory, as it was in high school. His professors only took roll call on the first few days of class. Students could just show up for tests and hand in their final papers if they so desired. It was a whole new, relaxed atmosphere. Michael had complete control of his own destiny. He was there because he wanted to be there. No one was forcing his hand.

He soon adjusted to the routine of college life; he buckled down and made frequent trips to the library to study. He made a bunch of new friends, though he never lost touch with Andrew, his oldest buddy, or Lauren, the love of his life.

She was always on his mind. The prom picture staring him in the face reminded him of her beauty day in and day out. As the days passed, Michael finally found time to sit down and write to her:

Dear Lauren,

I apologize for not writing sooner. It has been hectic around here, and I'm still settling into my new surroundings. My courses are already more challenging than they were in high school.

I'm starting to get into the swing of things, but I can't help but feel a little empty without you by my side. I think about you every day. Sometimes I wonder if I made the right decision going away to school rather than staying at home with you.

Please write me as often as you can. I want to hear about your senior year. I miss you.

Love,
Michael

Lauren and Michael wrote each other every week. The distance between them created some friction in their relationship, but they each kept their promises not to date anyone else.

From time to time, Lauren took the train up to Boston to spend the weekend. They visited downtown Boston together, shopped at the boutique stores, and ate at some gourmet restaurants. Some weekends, they checked into an inexpensive hotel so they could share some intimacy.

As freshman year flew by, Michael climbed to new heights. He gained an interest in writing and eventually advanced to chief editor of the school newspaper. He took advantage of the campus's vibrant social life by pledging a fraternity and moving into the frat house. It wasn't the neatest place, but the collegial atmosphere was unmatched. The fraternity members put aside their various backgrounds, tastes, and personalities in the name of brotherhood.

On the weekends, beer flowed from the kegs like waterfalls into a river. News of their parties spread like wildfire, and girls flocked to the excitement bursting from the house. Some danced to the music inside, while others huddled in small groups out on the lawn. Without Lauren at his hip, Michael had to shoo countless girls away. He was tempted at times but stayed true to his commitment.

Their interim separation motivated Lauren to follow in Michael's footsteps and enroll at Boston University. Although the school's rules required her to live in a dorm room, she spent nearly every weekend with Michael at the fraternity house. Now that they had reunited, Michael and Lauren fell even deeper in love.

While the happy couple flourished at college, bad news struck home in February of 1953. They received word that Nick was killed in the Korean War. Michael had a difficult time coping with the loss. He replayed the good times he had shared with Nick over and over in his mind, recalling their contentious stickball games and the day that Nick orchestrated their first viewing of pornography.

He envisioned Nick sitting beside him at the lunch table and driving that souped-up car he always tinkered with. He remembered the prom and Nick's bright smile when he announced that he was joining the Army after graduation. Michael found it hard to let go of these fond memories.

The immense loss was a rude awakening for Michael; he had never felt such emptiness inside. Losing a close friend enlightened him to the fragility of life. The memory of Nick would forever be etched in his mind. He was proud to call such a hero one of his best friends.

At the funeral, he reunited with his old buddies, Alan, Freddie, and Andrew. Tammy, Lauren, and some of their girlfriends also showed up to pay tribute at the honor guard funeral. Hugs and kisses were exchanged, but did little to help them cope with Nick's untimely death. During the service, they all made use of the tissues they clasped in their hands. Everyone except Michael.

But when the priest finished his speech by praising Nick's heroism and his unparalleled character, Michael couldn't hold it in any longer. Lauren casually slipped him a handful of tissues to wipe his tears. After the service, Nick's body was shipped to Arlington National Cemetery, where he was laid to rest at a private funeral held by the family.

As his senior year of college began, Michael sensed that it was time to move on to bigger and better things. As a finance major, Michael achieved outstanding grades and ranked at the top of his class. Through the on-campus recruiting process, he landed an entry-level position at Jones Bailey, a top-notch investment-banking firm on Wall Street.

Chapter 8

O n his graduation day in June of 1955, Michael truly felt a sense of accomplishment. Dressed in his cap and gown, he smiled from head to toe. Both his and Lauren's families surrounded him.

"Let me get a picture of you and Lauren," Becky cried out, waving her camera. "Just stay like that and say, 'cheese,'" she directed.

"Michael, let me get a picture of your entire family," Mr. Peterson said. "That's perfect," he proclaimed, as he snapped the photograph.

"Now let me get a picture of the Petersons," Becky countered.

"Hey! Can you take a picture of all of us?" Michael shouted to a gentleman walking nearby. The two families huddled together and posed for a group shot.

The highly anticipated hour finally arrived. Michael led all of his classmates down the aisle to a concerto played by the school orchestra. Since he was at the top of the class, Michael was given the honor to speak at the ceremony. He ascended the platform and took his seat onstage amongst the professors and special guests of honor.

The audience filled the entirety of the bleachers. The band played the national anthem, and everyone recited the Pledge of Allegiance. The Dean of the university and a distinguished guest speaker addressed the crowd. The Dean returned to the podium to introduce Michael, who rose and stepped towards the microphone.

"Distinguished guests of honor, faculty, and fellow members of the class of 1955, it is a great honor to stand before you today. In this crowd, I can see our country. People of all colors, religious affiliations, and political beliefs are in attendance. Despite our differences, we Americans have united together to defend our Constitution and the rights it guarantees us.

We have fought long and hard in too many wars to ensure that future generations will be able to enjoy the liberties that the Founding Fathers envisioned for our upstart nation. To those veterans here today, I salute each and every one of you for your courage and the sacrifices you've made to honor and protect our country's way of life.

Let us all learn from the lessons of war and come together to make a better world. Let us remove the word 'hate' from our vocabulary and obliterate all wars. We must replace evil with kindness, and conflict with peace. God bless America!"

The crowd roared in approval and gave Michael a standing ovation. Sadie and Herb were overwhelmed with pride after their son's eloquent speech.

The ceremony concluded with the announcement of the names of the graduating students. One by one, the graduates walked onstage to accept their diplomas. The Dean officially pronounced the graduation of the class of 1955, and the students threw their caps into the sky.

Lauren rushed onto the field and navigated through the crowd to find her love. When she finally spotted Michael, she dashed into his arms and clung to him like a vine wrapped around a branch. Tears of joy streamed down her cheeks.

"I'm so proud of you," she shouted over the raucous graduates. "Your speech was incredible. I love you."

"I love you too, Lauren."

Lauren couldn't wait to spend her future with him.

Chapter 9

At 6:30 AM, Michael's alarm clock blared, higher-pitched than a banshee's scream. Half awake, he pounded the snooze button so that he could squeeze in another couple of minutes before getting out of bed. His college days were long behind him; in the real world, he couldn't design his schedule to accommodate his personal sleeping habits.

Every morning he had to rush through his morning routine in order to catch the subway and make it to work on time. His outfit matched those of the Wall Street crowd; Michael wore a suit, bowtie, starched French-cuffed shirt, and dress pants held up by suspenders. Like his peers, he tried to keep up with New York's fast pace but, more often than not, nodded off on the train ride.

He had been working for nearly two weeks, but today was his first day on the trading floor. He'd meet his superior, Jerry Blankwell, for the first time.

"Hey Mike, let's get this show on the road," Jerry shouted, a cigar clenched firmly between his teeth. He beckoned Michael to his desk.

"Listen kid, as soon as the bell kicks off, the phones will be ringing off the hooks. So be prepared. The clients will ask you for stock quotes and place their buy and sell orders. If you can

42

execute—and keep them happy—you'll find success here. And then I'll be happy," he chuckled. "Just watch me."

Michael sat beside Jerry, and they waited for the trading day to get underway. At 9:30 on the dot, the phone rang, prompting Jerry to sit up straight in his chair and clear his throat. He snapped up the handset and signaled for Michael to pay close attention.

Michael had come prepared with a pad of paper and pen to take notes on his boss's process. A seasoned stockbroker for over twenty years, Jerry handled the call with what seemed like casual ease.

"The key is convincing them that you know what you're talking about," he advised Michael after hanging up with the client. "You'll get the hang of it after you field a bunch of calls. That'll come later. Today, you're the coffee and lunch man. I pay, you go. Does that work for you?"

Michael nodded yes. He could already sense that Jerry wanted the best for him.

For the remainder of the morning, chaos reigned. Phones rang off the hook, and the traders' chatter reverberated throughout the entire floor. Michael studied every move that Jerry made. After just one day of witnessing the billions of dollars transacted in the marketplace, he knew that he wanted a piece of the action.

"Michael, why don't you take a break?" Jerry suggested around noon. "Go out and get us some coffee and bagels." He handed Michael a 20-dollar bill. "Keep the change. That's your first decent tip of the day," he joked.

Michael took the money and ambled out of the office. He was slightly overwhelmed by his first experience in the financial world, but he wasn't deterred.

Day by day, slip by slip, and call by call, through trial and error, Michael got the gist of it. He was a fast learner and knew how to ask the right questions. He gained confidence in himself as Jerry took him under his wing and taught him how to obtain new clients. Before long, through hard work, dedication, and perseverance, he began to reap the rewards.

Michael developed his own list of clients and gained their respect. He advised them to make the right investments, which, more often than not, yielded great returns for their portfolios. With his polished appearance, ambition, and business savvy, he possessed the right ingredients to climb up the corporate ladder.

As time wore on, Michael and Jerry's relationship blossomed. They relished each other's company at corporate-sponsored golf outings, happy hours at the local bar, and the occasional lunch break. Since they developed quite the rapport, Michael felt comfortable confiding in his newfound mentor.

After a hard day's work, they often dropped by a cocktail lounge not too far from the office. It was a relaxing change of pace from riding out the highs and lows of the market all day. Kicking back with a few beers relieved them of the constant stress inherent to the financial world.

Michael and Jerry were regulars, on a first-name basis with the waitresses, who wore high heels, miniskirts, and low-cut tops that left little to the imagination.

On this typical Wednesday night, they sat at the bar, nursing their drinks and gazing at the crowd.

"How's Lauren been?" asked Jerry.

"She's doing great."

"When are you finally going to put a ring on her finger?"

"Funny you should ask. I just went down to jeweler's row the other night to look at stones and settings. Though I'm having difficulty deciding between an oval and a round cut stone. Do you know anything about jewelry? Normally I'd ask Lauren, but I want to surprise her."

"Hell no! I got the stone for Louise's ring from my late grandmother, so I didn't have much of a choice. I guess I'm lucky she adored it."

"Can I get you another drink?" the cocktail waitress interjected.

"What other beers do you have on tap?" Jerry asked.

"We have Schlitz, Ortlieb's, and Ballantine."

"Your choice, honey," Jerry said.

"And you, sir?"

"Makes no difference to me. They're all good," Michael answered.

Following the interruption, Michael switched gears. "I heard that GE might come out with a new engine that's faster and more efficient than the Rolls Royce's. The Air Force may take an option on it. I'm thinking of buying ten thousand shares."

"Just sit tight," Jerry advised him. "When we get back to the office, I'll put a call into John McGuire. He specializes in airline stocks, so he's real close with the director of R&D over there. If anybody knows, he'll know. I'll pick his brain out on the links. Maybe I'll end up buying some along with you," he said with a wink.

"Speaking of, how's your golf game been, Mike?"

"I can't seem to break 95," Michael griped. "I do okay on the front nine, but then I always seem to fizzle out on the back. Though I've been practicing: tapping a ball into a cup in my living room. I've also been spending some time at the driving range in Oceanside when I get the chance," he added.

"One of these days I'll bring you out to my country club for a round. I'll give you some pointers," Jerry suggested.

They finished their beers and called it a day.

Chapter 10

A black jewelry box sat on Michael's nightstand. The ring inside was screaming to come out and slide into place on Lauren's finger. Each night before going to bed, Michael racked his mind for a creative way to surprise her with a memorable proposal.

He could pop the question at a baseball game, take her to dinner in Little Italy, or revisit the banks of the Passaic, their old romantic enclave. But once he found a restaurant by the river's edge that had gotten a rave review in the paper, he knew he'd discovered the perfect setting. They could listen to the sounds of rumbling water and gaze at the passing boats as a small ensemble serenaded them with soft, romantic music.

He lured her there under the guise of celebrating her birthday.

"May I help you?" the maître d' asked from behind the podium.

"We have a reservation for two this evening. It's under Michael Aronstein."

"Oh yes," he said, scratching his name off the list. With a wave of his arm, the host instructed a waiter to escort them to a secluded area facing the river.

Michael and Lauren sat down at the round table, which was covered by a long white cloth. Rows of silverware sat upon cloth napkins, complementing the fine china and sparkling crystal glasses. Dimly lit candles accentuated the romantic ambiance. The waiters pulled out their chairs.

"My name is Pierre and this is my assistant, Clarke. We'll be at your service tonight. Here is our wine list."

Clarke handed them menus, placed a basket of bread in the center, and filled their glasses with water. After spreading the napkin on his thighs, Michael reached out to Lauren and clutched her hands.

"You look exquisite," he said, gazing into her eyes. Her silky blonde hair was pulled up, and she wore pearl earrings with a matching pearl necklace. "You light up the room," he added. She accepted the compliments with a gleaming smile.

"You don't look so bad yourself," she countered. Looking around, she said, "You're the handsomest guy here tonight." Michael smiled and kissed her awaiting lips.

They reached into the breadbasket and chose from the freshly baked selection. They dipped their knives into the butter and spread it on the rolls. Their warmth softened the butter, which seeped into the crevices of the bread.

"Have you spoken to Andrew lately?" she inquired.

"I talked to him the other day, but only briefly, since he's busy studying for his law school entrance exams."

"I spoke with some of my old girlfriends," Lauren added. "We may all get together to go shopping and have lunch next week."

"That sounds like fun."

Pierre approached the table and asked for their cocktail order.

"I have a great idea," Michael began. "Why don't we have a bottle of champagne to celebrate your big day?"

Lauren was surprised; she had never seen Michael order champagne. He usually drank red wine with dinner. Pierre instructed Clarke to prepare an ice bucket while he retrieved a bottle from the bar.

"Let's dance," Michael said, grabbing Lauren by the hand and guiding her to a small wooden dance floor. The four-piece band played a ballad for the couples that were dancing in the close quarters. Michael pressed Lauren's body to his as the saxophonist launched into a solo. He whispered, "I love you," into her ear and kissed her forehead, locking his arms around her waist.

The song concluded, and the couple returned to the table, where the champagne waited atop a bucket of ice. Pierre and Clarke, who waited nearby, had neatly refolded their napkins and placed them beside their plates. Michael and Lauren took their seats, and Pierre popped the cork on the champagne bottle, releasing a cool mist into the air. He poured the sparkling wine into their champagne flutes.

"To the love of my life," Michael toasted, as their glasses touched with a chime.

"Mm-m this tastes good," Lauren remarked after her first sip. "It has a sweet aftertaste."

"Not as sweet as you," Michael said.

"You sure have a way with words," she cooed, smiling and clutching his hands. "And you're pretty sweet yourself," she added.

"May I take your order?" Pierre interjected.

"Can you give us another minute?" Michael requested, picking up the leather-bound menu for the first time.

"Michael, this menu is pricy."

"Don't worry about it. Just order to your heart's content," he insisted.

Michael and Lauren both ordered the surf and turf: lobster tail and filet mignon. Soon after, Lauren politely excused herself to the bathroom.

When she was out of sight, Michael whispered instructions to Pierre on how to surprise Lauren with the engagement ring. He removed the jewelry box from his sport jacket pocket and told the dutiful waiter, "Before you bring out the cake, slide this ring over the sparkler in the center." Pierre smiled and nodded his head in acknowledgement just as Lauren returned to her seat.

They began with salad and then dug into the main course. Before ordering dessert, they walked out onto the deck overlooking the river. The moon glowed and the stars twinkled; the Big Dipper lit up the sky. There was a little breeze blowing off the swiftly flowing waters. Michael draped his jacket over Lauren's shoulders to ease the chill. It was romantic and peaceful, reminiscent of the many moments they had spent by the water in the previous six years.

"It's just beautiful out here," Lauren announced.

"It certainly is," Michael agreed. "I'd like to have a house overlooking the water someday."

"You and I think alike," she responded. "Michael, where do you think we'll be ten years from now?"

"I'll keep you pregnant every year."

"No, seriously, Michael."

"I see myself in a big, beautiful home with a gorgeous wife by my side. And maybe three kids and a dog to keep us company."

She cuddled closer to him, wrapping her arm around his waist. Michael escorted Lauren back inside and sat back down at the table. To preserve the forthcoming surprise, Michael and Pierre conducted the usual repartee of ordering dessert.

Clarke brought them some coffee, and, a few minutes later, a beautiful cake with a glistening sparkler in the center. A group of waiters sang 'Happy Birthday' to Lauren, and some nearby diners joined in. Lauren sat quietly, blushing as she admired the magnificent cake.

"Make a wish," Michael instructed. She closed her eyes for a moment and blew out the candles, not yet recognizing the diamond ring in the middle. When she reopened them, she inspected the cake's decorative details and noticed a sparkling, glass-like substance in the center.

After a moment, she let out a scream and scooped it off the pastry. She placed the rock on her finger with a joyful squeal and leaned over the table to give Michael a kiss. He stooped down to one knee and asked Lauren to marry him. Her emotions got the best of her; she could only nod her head up and down through the tears. Practically the whole restaurant witnessed the momentous occasion. Lauren had gotten her knight in shining armor, and Michael captured his princess.

Lauren was bursting at the seams; she couldn't wait to share her good news with the world.

"Mom, Dad, are you awake?" she screamed, running through the front door of her parents' house.

Alarmed, her mother shouted back, "Is everything alright?"

"Come on out. Michael and I are here. We have big news!"

Still half asleep, her parents emerged from their bedroom in matching robes.

"Mom, look!" Lauren proudly extended her finger and showed off her sparkling diamond ring.

"That is just beautiful," Mrs. Peterson remarked. "Let me look a little closer."

"Can I take a peek?" her father requested. "Wow! That is some rock."

"Welcome to the family," Lauren's mother said, as she hugged Michael and kissed him on the cheek.

"Congratulations, Michael," Victor said. He reached out to shake his future son in-law's hand.

"Isn't it gorgeous?" Lauren exclaimed. "The stone is so big, you can see each and every facet!"

"Yes," her mother added. "And the shape and setting really accentuate the diamond."

At Michael's family's celebratory brunch the following morning, Sadie Aronstein set down a tray of lox, herring, bagels, and eggs on her kitchen table. She ran over and gave Lauren a warm embrace as soon as she walked through the door.

"Let me see the ring," she cried out. "Oh my God, it's gorgeous."

"Let me see, Mom," Becky yelled, as she entered from the living room. "Wow!"

"That must have cost you a pretty penny," Herbie joked. Michael's father wasn't accustomed to such extravagant jewelry; he'd always preferred a good bargain.

"Come sit down," Sadie directed.

"Let's toast to the bride and groom. May they have a beautiful life together," Herb bellowed, as everyone lifted their champagne glasses in the air. He continued, "You know this champagne bottle is from your Bar Mitzvah. Your mother and I have been waiting a long time to open it. And today is certainly the perfect day."

"So tell me, when do you two expect to tie the knot?" Sadie asked.

"Well, we haven't talked about it yet," Lauren explained, turning to Michael for his reaction. "But I think I'd like to have a June wedding. It's the perfect time of the year."

"I agree," said Michael.

"Do you know where you'd like to be married?" his mother went on.

"I've thought about having it at my church," said Lauren. That answer did not bode too well with the observant Aronsteins. Interfaith marriage was rare in their family.

"We'll have to talk about that," Michael cut in, looking at both his parents as to assure them that he would handle it.

"Let's eat," his mother said with a smile, successfully moving away from the potentially sticky subject.

As they ate, they continued to talk about their future plans until a phone ring interrupted the conversation. Lauren's mother had called to congratulate Michael's parents on the engagement and invite them over to the house for a formal dinner. The women exchanged congratulatory words and worked out the details of the dinner plans.

The meal concluded, and they all exchanged loving farewells. But during the ride home, Michael and Lauren got into a heated argument.

"You don't understand, Lauren! I don't particularly care where we get married. I would marry you anywhere on earth. It just wouldn't be fair to my family. A lot of our guests are religious and would refuse to attend a ceremony held in a church. We'll have to find some common ground."

"I've always dreamed of having a church wedding, Michael. Please don't take that away from me."

"I guess we still have a lot to discuss," Michael said. "What about our children? What religion will they practice?"

"Mine, of course," Lauren dismissively replied.

Chapter 11

That next Monday morning at work, Michael was anxious to announce his engagement. Word quickly spread around the office, and virtually all of his coworkers stopped by his desk to express their congratulations and well wishes.

As Michael shuffled through some unanswered messages from the previous week, one particular slip caught his attention. It was from Jonathon Steinhardt's secretary. The president of the company wanted to meet with him.

Since Steinhardt had never before contacted him directly, the first thought that popped into Michael's mind was that he was being fired. Though he couldn't come up with anything that he'd done wrong.

He contacted Jerry to see if he had any explanation, but his boss was just as puzzled. With a knot in his stomach, Michael returned Steinhardt's call and set up an appointment for the following day.

Despite this unforeseen distraction, Michael finished out the workday in good spirits. But as he traveled home that night, he couldn't stop worrying. He couldn't afford to lose his job, especially now that he was engaged. What would Lauren say?

He opted to keep the information from her until he got a better handle on the situation himself.

The following morning, Michael entered Jonathon Steinhardt's office, noticeably wary of the prospect of meeting such a legend. Practically a celebrity on Wall Street, Steinhardt had a staggering financial track record. When he spoke, people listened.

Preoccupied with a telephone conversation, Jonathon motioned for Michael to take a seat. Michael stepped into the huge, lavishly decorated office, furnished with a leather sofa, giant conference table, mahogany executive desk, and expensive paintings mounted on the Roman-etched paneled wood walls. His feet practically sank into the plush carpeting.

Steinhardt, a distinguished gentleman with salt and pepper hair, sat behind the desk. His diamond-studded, initialed cufflinks protruded from the sleeves of his suit jacket.

Sitting patiently in one of the two leather armchairs facing Jonathon, Michael admired the numerous framed family photos that sat on the desk before him. The snapshots of Steinhardt's adventures sailing around the globe added another dimension to the man's character.

As Michael's eyes wandered, he couldn't help but notice the meticulousness with which Steinhardt's desk was arranged. There wasn't a single piece of paper out of sorts. Its rigid formation called to mind a drill team standing at attention. A box of tissues was perched on the edge of the desk, ostensibly to ensure that if any speckles of dust appeared on the surface, Jonathon could easily wipe it clean.

"Sorry about that," Steinhardt apologized. He hung up the phone and shook Michael's hand. "Can I get you some coffee or tea?"

"I'll have some coffee. Thank you."

Jonathon instructed his secretary to pour them two cups of coffee. She shuffled over to the built-in bar, which held a set of china cups, saucers, and a sterling silver coffee pot.

"Let's start with the big picture. So—how's it going, Michael?"

"It's going quite well. I've been turning in significant profits ever since—"

"Do you like what you're doing here?" Steinhardt interjected.

"Very much so," Michael assured him.

"That's precisely why you're here. In my office, that is. You might not be aware of this, but I've been observing you very closely since you started on the floor. And I must say, you've brought in an astounding number of clients and generated a corresponding amount of business. Such stellar performance by someone at your age is unprecedented here at Jones Bailey. You've won the 500-meter dash by a mile. Everyone else— they're left in the dust."

Steinhardt sat up in his chair, meeting Michael's eyes.

"What I'm saying, Michael, is that you deserve some sort of a gold medal—in the form of a promotion."

"Well, thank you, sir," Michael replied. He had no clue how to follow up on that metaphor.

"No, thank you. You've done a wonderful job."

"What kind of promotion do you have in mind?" Michael asked.

"I've been planning to open up a new division: Mergers and Acquisitions. It's still in an early stage, but I think you and your talents will fit in quite well once we get it up and running."

"That sounds interesting. Can you go into a little more detail?"

"It'll entail a boatload of relationship-building with new clients, something you have a knack for."

"Can I keep my existing clients?"

"No way," he chuckled. "But you won't need them once you start running with the big guns. No more Mom & Pops trying to build up a nice little nest egg for the family. We're talking big! All those corporations listed on the exchanges—they'll be your new clients."

"That sounds fantastic. But how do I make money? Are these companies trading stocks at a much larger scale?"

"No, this is much different from the game you're in now. You'll be convincing the big boys to contract our firm to raise the capital needed to acquire or merge with other companies. These kinds of deals usually amount to hundreds of millions of dollars, and we'll receive a percentage of the gross capital raised. You'll get a percentage of that."

"Don't companies usually acquire these types of loans from the banks?"

"Exactly. We want to go after that business. We think that we can do it just as well, if not better, than the banks. I know it's a risk, but how do you think I got here?" He spun around in his desk chair and basked in glory of his pristine office.

"I'm confident you're the man for the job. What do you think?"

"It sounds like a great opportunity, Mr. Steinhardt, but—"

"Call me Jonathon."

"But it'll be difficult to walk away from all of my clients. They trust me."

"You were so successful with these small guys, just think of what you could do on a larger scale. The money will far exceed what you're making now. Besides, we'll continue to pay your current salary in addition to all of your travel and entertainment expenses. You don't have to worry about a thing. Jerry will take over your existing accounts, if that's any consolation."

"Oh, wow. Jerry's not coming with me?"

"No, sir. Plain and simple—*you* are just what we're looking for. A youthful, polished image. Those kind of attributes make more of a difference than you might think."

"I'm honored," Michael replied.

"Rest assured that as soon as this takes off, you'll be able to hire other salespeople and take an override from their commissions as well. Think of all those big fat bonus checks."

Steinhardt's sales pitch was impressive; the man oozed business acumen. Michael analyzed the downside risk and determined that he was still young enough to survive in the event of a failure. Besides, he figured, it would add more experience to his already impressive resume. Michael graciously accepted the position and gave Jonathon a strong handshake.

Elated, Michael set up a lunch with Jerry to discuss his new position. Michael found him situated at the bar, sipping on a drink as he waited. Jerry waved his hand and gestured to the vacant seat next to him.

"Sit down, Mike. What are you drinking? Let's celebrate."

"I'd rather celebrate at a table, if you don't mind," Michael said.

"No problem."

Michael ordered a draft beer and they sat down in a booth.

"So explain to me what this new position is all about."

"It's part of a new startup division called Mergers and Acquisitions," Michael began.

"What is that?" Jerry asked, as if it were a foreign language.

59

Michael parroted Jonathon's spiel the best he could for his trusted boss, who caught on almost immediately.

"You'd better get your golf game up to snuff," Jerry insisted.

"Why's that?"

"Cause more deals are made out there on the fairways than at the office." Jerry snickered. "Why don't you finally come over to my club? We can shoot a couple rounds, and I can even get you some private lessons with a pro."

"I'll definitely take you up on that," he promised.

But before Michael could finish his thought, his eyes locked onto the voluptuous, mini-skirted cocktail waitress sashaying over to their table in stiletto heels. Jerry was mesmerized as well. They couldn't help but stare, imagining what was underneath that dress.

"You new around here?" asked Jerry. "Never seen you before."

"No, I usually work the late shift. I'm filling in for someone who called in sick," she clarified.

"What's your name?" asked Michael.

"Maria," she answered with a flirtatious wink. After taking their orders, she strolled away with a deliberate sway of her behind.

"Some piece of ass!" Jerry exclaimed, as she disappeared into the kitchen.

"Haven't seen too many bods like that floating around," Michael added.

"She's got the eye out for you, buddy. Watch out!"

Michael wasn't sure if he was being serious.

"They can tell if a guy's married, you know. Or, in your case, set to be married."

"So what?" Michael retorted.

"Look kid, we get along pretty well at work, but I don't know much about your personal life." Jerry cleared his throat. "The thing is, getting hitched is a bigger commitment than you realize. You're not just committed to your gal, you've also gotta be committed to avoiding the ones like her." He nodded in Maria's direction. "A young successful guy like you, you better be on your toes. You can look, but don't touch."

"You've got me all wrong, Jerry—" Michael protested.

"I know, I know. You're a good guy. So am I. But after fifteen years of marriage, waking up next to the same woman every morning, I can't help but fantasize about all these broads. All of 'em."

Chapter 12

The Petersons and Aronsteins prepared for their big celebratory dinner. They hadn't all spent much time together since Michael's college graduation. Although Michael and Lauren dated for many years, their families had never become too well acquainted. Michael kept them at bay because, as far as he was concerned, they had little in common. He never felt the need to force the relationship while he and Lauren were only dating. But now they were engaged to be married.

Michael and his family arrived at the front door of the Petersons' home.

"Come in, come in. So happy to see you," Lauren greeted them. She gave Michael a peck on his lips and hugged his parents and sister. Hospitality was her trademark.

Lauren's family gathered behind her and matched her warm reception with their own hugs and smiles.

"Let's celebrate!" Victor shouted, starting off the party. "What are you drinking?" he asked the Aronstein family.

He directed them to the living room, where a credenza displayed bottles of alcohol.

"I'll have a vodka on the rocks," Herbie said.

"And for you, Sadie?"

"Red wine would be great."

Victor poured the drinks and addressed the group. "May I have your attention," he shouted, tapping a spoon to a crystal glass. "Let's raise our glasses to Michael and Lauren. And also to Michael's big promotion."

They lifted their glasses in the air and toasted the occasion. Michael took an especially large gulp of his vodka tonic.

Lauren's mother served numerous platters of hors d'oeuvres that she had worked so hard to prepare the night before. Her extra effort paid off, since everyone raved about the food.

"You have to give me some of those recipes," Sadie insisted.

"I got them from this fabulous new cookbook. I'll show it to you later on. It has so many great recipes," Martha told her.

On the other side of the room, Herbie admired some of the family pictures hung on the wall. Victor walked up beside him, prompting Herbie to initiate some conversation.

"I see you like to sail."

"Yes, indeed. My greatest passion," Victor said. "Besides my wife, of course."

"Naturally," added Herbie.

"But if I could sail around the world for the rest of my life, I'd do it in a heartbeat. I ask Martha for permission twice a week," he laughed.

"Michael's told me about his time on your boat. He's growing to love the sport, too."

"Your son's a great sailor. Has a knack for knowing just when to catch the wind at its optimum speed. You gotta recognize talent when you see it."

Martha and Sadie, who chatted about some of the Petersons' decorative furniture, were also becoming more comfortable in each other's company.

After taking a tour of the house, the families gathered at the dining room table for the meal. Martha had spent the entire week pondering what to prepare before deciding on her special apple-baked ham with all the fixings. Halfway through her preparation, however, she remembered that the Aronsteins maintained a kosher diet. So she made a roasted chicken and matzo ball soup to complete the menu. It was important to respect their Jewish culture in addition to providing a delicious meal.

"Everything looks so appetizing," commented Sadie.

"It smells good, too," added Becky.

"Well, let's eat and discuss some of these wedding plans," Victor said, taking the initiative. "I know that Lauren has her heart set on having the wedding at our church. What do you think of that?"

Michael took it upon himself to speak for his family. "I love Lauren, and the last thing that I want to do is hurt her. But having the wedding in a church may cause some of our other guests discomfort, especially the religious ones."

"Our families wouldn't mind attending a ceremony in a synagogue," Martha countered.

"But it's different for them," Michael stressed.

"Well, then what do you propose, Michael?" Victor asked, respectfully.

"I think that we should have the wedding in a neutral place, such as a hall or country club. That would help to alleviate some of our guests' concerns. I also think that someone secular, like a judge, should officiate the ceremony. That would satisfy everybody, no matter the religion. It's fair and it's the right thing to do," he concluded.

Despite Michael's pragmatism, the families did not come to an agreement as to where the wedding would take place. They all finished dinner and said their farewells, leaving the decision up in the air.

Chapter 13

At his new position in Mergers and Acquisitions, Michael was expected to work long hours and travel all over the country to introduce himself to key executives. Planting the seeds for future investment opportunities was an integral part of the firm's plans to get the new division up and running.

He couldn't rest on the laurels of his past success any longer. He had to get the word out about this new venture. His effectiveness would now be gauged solely by his ability to generate new business for the firm. Although he was quite familiar with the old adage, "You're only as good as your last sale," Michael felt confident in his ability to succeed in this new endeavor.

He did expect to encounter some pitfalls, though. He wondered if accepting a new job in the midst of planning a wedding was the right choice, since he wouldn't be able to spend as much time at home with Lauren

She would be left all alone for much of the week. Though he felt a little guilty, Michael rationalized the situation, assuring Lauren that his new position offered an incredible opportunity to build a future for their family. Plus, he'd be around on the weekends.

On his first business trip, Michael couldn't get a good night's rest. He lied in the stiff bed, staring up at the chipped ceiling of the motel room. Dallas already seemed like a foreign country, and all he'd done was take a cab ride from the airport to the motel. So much open space, populated with only cacti, like nothing he'd ever seen in New York.

As he tossed and turned, Michael's thoughts accelerated: how would he close this deal? Midwest Electronics was expecting a comprehensive presentation on his new division, and it was Michael's job to talk up all the benefits and convince them to play ball.

He'd had a few genial conversations with James O'Hanley, the CFO of Midwest, over the phone and was curious to meet the gravelly-voiced man in person. Michael was fairly confident that they'd get on just as well once they were in the same room, but some doubt still lingered in the back of his mind.

The pressure was getting to him. Since receiving the promotion, Michael had exhausted himself, putting in a slew of overtime hours of research to support the new venture. His and Steinhardt's reputations were on the line; Jonathon made sure to remind him of that.

Michael lifted his head and flipped the pillow over. He thought about Lauren's pet peeve about cold pillows. She couldn't stand them. Sometimes Michael would have to lie on hers while she finished in the bathroom just to warm it up. He grinned to himself and plopped his face back down onto the bag of feathers. If it weren't so late back in New York, he'd have called her. Lauren's mellifluous tone could always put him to sleep.

He awoke at 9:00 AM to slivers of sunlight piercing through the drawn shades. This is it, he thought to himself. The day that could change everything. Within moments, he realized that he didn't have much time to get ready. The appointment was at 10:30, and he still had to wash up, check out, and catch a cab to the office.

There was no use in waiting for the water to heat up. Michael braved the cold shower, then hopped out for a quick shave, during which he nicked himself underneath the chin. He tore off a square of tissue paper and dabbed the cut as he slithered into his trousers. After quickly gathering his belongings—he didn't have many—he zipped the suitcase shut, buttoned up his shirt, and hustled down to the lobby to check out.

To his dismay, he had to wait for the clerk to call a taxi and for the actual car to arrive. Precious minutes were ticking away. Fortunately, Michael didn't have to wait long. The driver pulled into the motel parking lot and unlocked the door. Michael hopped in the back and relayed the address of Midwest Electronics. The cabbie knew it well; their huge complex was visible from the highway.

In the daylight, Michael was even more attune to the expansive landscape surrounding the heart of the city. He stared out the window until they arrived at the isolated cluster of buildings about which the driver spoke.

Michael handed him a 20-dollar bill and insisted that he keep the change—the company would reimburse him anyhow. He entered the main building's lobby, which showcased a variety of southwestern décor. Michael was intrigued by the prevailing style of the region, but couldn't stop to admire it right then and there. He approached a receptionist and gave his name, as well as O'Hanley's.

He was instructed to sign the guest register and affix a nametag while he waited for Mr. O'Hanley to come down to greet him. He'd never walked into a meeting with a nametag back in New York, but Michael wasn't certain of the appropriate business etiquette down in Texas. He carefully scrawled his name onto the front, peeled off the back label, and pressed the sticker onto his breast pocket.

At the light ding of the elevator, Michael looked up to see an older, plain Jane-looking woman walking towards him.

"You must be Michael Aronstein," she surmised, extending her hand.

"How'd you know?" Michael joked, gesturing to his nametag. The woman laughed. He was off to a good start.

"I'm Peggy Simpson, Mr. O'Hanley's secretary. How was your flight in from New York?"

"Fine, thank you," Michael replied.

They entered the elevator and rode up to the top floor of the building. The doors opened to reveal an ornately decorated corridor that led to just one office. Its munificence reminded him of his meeting with Jonathon, when the Mergers & Acquisitions division was first brought to his attention.

"Please have a seat while I let Mr. O'Hanley know you're here."

Waiting patiently, Michael thumbed through some of the magazines that sat atop the coffee table by his feet. Issues of *Look Magazine*, *Life*, some technical publications, and industry-specific trade newsletters made up the collection. Michael picked up one of the newsletters, looking to brush up on some technical jargon at the last moment. Luckily, the front page of the one he chose featured an article on Midwest Electronics.

The headline noted that the company was poised for expansion and needed to raise more capital for a new plant and the requisite equipment. Demand for its' products were soaring overseas, and Midwest couldn't keep up with the orders. Michael had come across this information in his preparatory research, but rereading the article nevertheless gave him an extra boost of confidence before the presentation.

Peggy ushered him into O'Hanley's office and directed him to the open chair across from her boss, who stood to shake Michael's hand. James O'Hanley looked quite similar to what Michael had envisioned: tall, slender, and exquisitely dressed in a bowtie, vest, and pointed cowboy boots.

"Sorry about the strong grip, son," O'Hanley boomed, "but that's just how we do thangs down here in Texas."

"Of course, sir. I appreciate the enthusiasm."

"Same here," he said, pointing to Michael's nametag. "As if I didn't know who you were," he chuckled. Michael grinned sheepishly and self-consciously touched the sticker.

"So tell me a little bit about yourself and the firm, Michael. Your introductory letter was impressive, but I'd like to hear it 'straight from the horse's mouth', as we say down here in Texas."

"Sir, they say that everywhere," Peggy chimed in.

"Thank you, Peggy. You can leave now," O'Hanley barked.

"Well, sir," Michael started.

"Please, call me Jim."

"Alright, Jim. To sum it up, we're young and aggressive. We can work harder and smarter than the other guys—pretty much kick some ass, if you know what I mean."

"That's great. But be more specific. What can Jones Bailey do for me that your competitors can't?"

"I can offer you lower fees, to start." Michael offered.

"That's great. Keep going."

"And since we have access to investors both domestic and abroad, our firm will be able to raise a cheaper cost of capital."

"I've got to be honest, Michael, I like what I'm hearing. So would we work with you alone, or also with your superiors?"

"I'll handle the day-to-day business, but my boss, Jonathon Steinhardt, will consult with me on the big picture outlook. Have you heard of Jonathon?"

"Of course. The Prince of Wall Street. In fact, we went to college together." Michael lit up—this deal seemed like a sure thing.

"Wow. That'd be great if we could all do some business."

O'Hanley took a long pause as he mulled over his response.

"Let's get that old whipper snapper on the phone," he announced with a grin. "I'll take a look at some of the numbers your office sent over, and then we'll make this official."

Chapter 14

*W*hile Michael made presentations to major corporations, Lauren stayed busy, teaching her kindergarten class and making plans for the wedding. He occasionally felt lonely on the road, moving from one hotel to the next before he could even get comfortable. He had to fill in the gaps somehow.

Enjoying a drink at the bar often helped to pass the time. Sometimes he'd scan through pornographic magazines and construct elaborate fantasies in his head. Sex was constantly on his mind as it was, and being away from his future wife only exacerbated his natural urges.

On occasion, he'd venture out to a strip joint to fulfill the heightened sexual drive. He couldn't help but enjoy the strange satisfaction of stuffing dollar bills into the breasts or behinds of scantily clad strippers. One night, after a few too many gin and tonics, Michael was approached by a particularly svelte young vixen. Michael couldn't resist her invitation to the private back room for a lap dance, so he silently took her hand and followed her through a dark corridor into a palatial, velvet-lined space.

"You're adorable," she cooed, churning her ass into Michael's lap.

These forays to the titty bars were a man's thing, a dark side that he concealed from Lauren. What she didn't know couldn't hurt her. Besides, he wasn't cheating on her. It was merely to pass the time. He often encountered other traveling businessmen at these joints, and they justified it the exact same way. Considering how hard he worked during the day, he felt like he deserved the opportunity to blow off some steam.

Michael's perseverance eventually paid off, and he began to reap the fruits of his labor—a barrage of phone calls and inquiries about his new department. He could hardly find time to field all of the calls. Everyone requested to speak to Michael. He came off as likable, trustworthy, and impressively knowledgeable in his sales pitches.

Developing these relationships was a key ingredient to Michael's success. Jonathon Steinhardt wholeheartedly supported him; Michael's expense account was proof of that. Michael understood that the easiest way into someone's pocketbook was through the stomach, so he spared no expense to wine and dine his clients at the finest restaurants. Thanks to Jerry, Michael's newly sharpened golf skills enabled him to casually conduct business on the links, as well.

Motivated and conscientious, he'd rearrange his schedule and catch the next flight out of town to close a deal if the situation required it. More than willing to deal with such sacrifices, Lauren fended for herself much of the workweek. Anything to support her fiancé's success. Michael had always dreamed about the better things in life, and now his fantasies were coming true.

As his new venture grew and turned greater profits, he began to stay at nicer hotels, dine at more expensive restaurants, and fly first-class to his various destinations. He orchestrated some very big deals, which netted the firm huge profits and positioned them as a major player in the industry. The Mergers and Acquisitions division showed promise, but Michael knew that it could not sustain real growth so long as he was its only member. He recommended that the company hire new employees for him to take under his wing.

Chapter 15

*I*t was June of 1958, and the weather was perfect for a wedding. Before the guests arrived, the photographers snapped pictures of the two families.

An array of different colored flowers, articulately arranged in a landscaped design, surrounded the entrance to the country club. The white and pink buds of the flowering dogwood trees enveloped the walkway, and the chirping of birds filled the air as both families' guests arrived and assembled outside. They sat on white chairs that faced the chupah, a decorated marriage canopy, which was tastefully draped with matching white and pink roses. A judge waited under the canopy as a string of violins serenaded the audience with classical concertos.

The ceremony began, and a flower girl hopped down the aisle, sprinkling rose petals over the silky white fabric below. The ushers and bridesmaids followed.

Next, Michael's proud mother and father escorted him into the marital canopy. Lauren, equally nervous and excited, patiently waited for the cue to take her final steps into Michael's awaiting arms.

"This is it. How do I look, Mom?" she asked one last time.

"You look gorgeous."

Lauren smiled and dabbed her twinkling eyes with a tissue to expel the tears of joy. As she walked down the aisle, the guests expressed their utter amazement at her beauty and her magnificent bridal gown. She reached Michael's side, and Victor lifted his daughter's veil. The Petersons each kissed their daughter on the cheek. More tears streamed down Lauren's face–some of joy, some of sorrow. She was leaving the comfort and security of her parents' home to forge a new life of her own.

During the ceremony, all eyes were focused on the bride and groom. An overwhelming joy filled the room; everyone was elated to celebrate Michael and Lauren's union.

They exchanged vows after Andrew, the best man, presented the wedding bands. Cheers and applause echoed throughout the hall as the sun set in the pink and blue sky. With beaming smiles, the happy couple strode down the walkway for the very first time as husband and wife.

During the cocktail hour, complete with butlered hors d'oeuvres, many of the guests congratulated the newlyweds with hugs and kisses. The photographers kept snapping away.

"Where are you guys going on your honeymoon?" asked an inquisitive guest.

"Niagara Falls. We can't wait to get there," Lauren responded, squeezing her husband's hand.

"Lauren, come over here, honey," her mother called out over the noisy crowd. "I want to introduce you to a dear old friend of mine from grade school. This is Jane Mackerby, the girlfriend I always talked about who lives in Florida."

"Oh yeah," Lauren vaguely recalled.

"Oh my god, you're gorgeous," Jane complimented the bride. "She resembles you, Martha, only prettier," she chuckled. "For God's sake, you look just like a movie star, young lady."

"And this is her handsome husband, Michael," Martha added.

"What an adorable couple! Congratulations to both of you."

"Michael, come over here," his father interrupted. "I want to introduce you to a very special person. Do you remember Ann Wilson?"

"Yes, I remember hearing the name somewhere," he said.

"She's the stork who dropped you off at our home after your birth."

"You turned out to be such a handsome boy," Ann said. "And your wife is just stunning. Good luck to the both of you."

Puzzled, Lauren pulled Michael aside and whispered, "What does he mean by 'stork'? Were you adopted? Why didn't you tell me?"

"I don't know. It's not really a big deal. I guess it never crossed my mind. Besides, this isn't the time for that stuff. It's our wedding night. Let's enjoy the party." To his relief, Lauren smiled and pulled him over to a group of her coworkers.

Michael and Lauren couldn't step two feet without being stopped by friends or family members eager to congratulate and compliment them. The cocktail hour flew by, and neither Michael nor Lauren found time to taste the delicacies carried around by the wait staff.

The lights flickered, signaling that the cocktail hour was about to conclude. The guests were ushered to their awaiting tables as the band blasted their horns, inviting everyone to boogie the night away on the dance floor.

The floor was packed with a mixture of guests from both families, including some of Michael's ultra-religious relatives. After the first song ended, the bandleader announced the bridal party. A roar of applause reverberated throughout the room as the new Mr. and Mrs. Aronstein entered arm-in-arm. The band launched into the traditional Hora tune, and the crowd joined arms in a huge circle. Lauren and Michael stepped into the middle and sat down on adjacent chairs. Some of the stronger men lifted the chairs and raised them up and down. Exhilarated, Michael and Lauren shared a laugh as they both held on to a table napkin. They nearly touched the ceiling.

After the dance, Michael and Lauren sat on a heart-shaped bench positioned at the back center of the room, facing the band and other tables. Friends and relatives made brief toasts, but they were just the warm up for Andrew, the best man. Michael and Lauren listened intently to his prepared words. There was complete silence as their cherished friend addressed the crowd.

"For those of you who don't know me, I'm Andrew, Michael's best man and the brother he never had. Our friendship dates back to kindergarten and has only grown stronger through the years. We had a ton of fun times together, from attending birthday parties to playing spin the bottle in the basement with our friends."

He looked up from his notes. "Do you remember Babs, Michael?" Michael laughed and nodded his head.

"Our stickball games out in the streets were intense, but you always took it way more seriously than anyone else. I'll admit it—I was jealous of your skills with that sawed-off broomstick bat and pimpled ball. We got in some trouble now and then, but it never really amounted to much. We even dated girls together, and I've gotta say, you went out with some real doozies." The entire audience erupted in laughter.

"But there was that one special date, your first with your lovely new wife, Lauren. I remember the day you met her at your locker, the first day of senior year. It was immediately clear that you had fallen head-over-heels. Since she was the new girl in town, every guy in school stood in line for a chance to get their grubby hands on her. But you pulled it off and convinced her that you were the best game in town. I'm so happy for the both of you and thrilled to celebrate this special day in your lives. Let us all raise our glasses to the most beautiful couple on the planet."

Michael and Lauren rushed onto the dance floor and thanked Andrew for the kind words. Champagne flowed for the remainder of the affair, and the guests danced well into the night. Relishing this taste of the finer things life had to offer, Michael swore to himself that he'd somehow provide Lauren with such decadence for the rest of their lives together.

Chapter 16

Michael and Lauren settled down in Oceanside, New York after their wedding. They used the proceeds of their wedding gifts to buy their first home and start a new life as a family. Oceanside was a wonderful place to raise a family, just outside of the congestion and bustling life of Manhattan, yet still close enough that they could spontaneously steal off to enjoy the glitz and glamour of the city.

Living close to their families was another convenience. Lauren taught kindergarten at the local elementary school, while Michael continued working his way up Wall Street's corporate ladder. He didn't mind commuting to the city on a daily basis. Just a part of life.

Lauren soon got pregnant with a baby girl, whom they named Abbey. Michael was doing well enough to support them, so Lauren stopped teaching. She acquainted herself with their town and came to treat it as home rather quickly.

One sunny afternoon, Lauren took Abbey, now two years old, to a playground with a brand new swing set. As Lauren gently glided her daughter into the sky, another mother placed her child on the adjacent swing.

"How old is she?" asked the stranger.

"Just turned two."

"Isn't that funny, my daughter is the same age. How cute! Do you live around here?" she pressed.

"We live over by Elm Road, near St. Mary's Church."

"Oh, isn't that funny. I live on Stump Drive, on the other side of the church."

"We're practically neighbors," Lauren exclaimed.

"By the way, I'm Toby."

"Lauren. Nice to meet you," she said.

"Nice to meet you, too," Toby replied.

"Do you come here often?"

"I do. I like getting Danielle out of the house now and then. Besides, she loves the swings."

"She's precious."

"Thank you. What's your little munchkin's name?"

"Abbey. Abbey Aronstein."

The conversation continued, and the women discovered that they had mutual acquaintances, as well as a number of other things in common. They both had interfaith marriages and husbands who commuted into the city. Sensing that they seemed to mesh like the threads of a tightly woven fabric, Toby and Lauren exchanged phone numbers. It was the beginning of what would become a close relationship.

Toby and Lauren went shopping on the avenue, planned birthday parties, and arranged social events for their families. Since she had lived in Oceanside for practically all of her life, Toby was able to introduce Lauren to a whole slew of her friends. They all took turns hosting dinner parties and potluck dinners. Feeling like a part of the old gang, Michael and Lauren thoroughly enjoyed life in the new neighborhood.

With Jonathon's blessing, Michael began to expand his newly formed division. His business sense and intuition about people led him to hire a young upstart named Robert Jorgensen. Michael held a dozen interviews, and Bob proved to be the best candidate for the job. In addition to possessing the required corporate credentials, he was a WASP and would relate better to the stiff-collared conservative executives in corporate America. Michael valued religious diversity, plus he liked Bob's energy and eagerness to learn the ropes. Like Michael, he was married and had a young child.

Michael's time was still stretched thin even after Jorgenson came aboard. He was burning the candle at both ends; it was challenging to simultaneously maintain his business and train a new employee. Michael had Bob shadow him for a week to learn how to attract new clients to the firm. Bob admired Michael's talents and hung on his every word.

Michael expected a lot from his protégé. If Bob failed to produce, Jonathan could pull the plug on their new division without blinking an eye. Michael worked closely with his latest hire, discussing business over lunch on a regular basis. They also socialized outside of the office and became close friends.

Together, they worked tirelessly to achieve success for the Mergers and Acquisitions division. The business continued to grow, and Michael's schedule became even more hectic. The action on Wall Street dominated most of his time.

Meanwhile, Lauren excelled in her role as a mother and wife. She remained upbeat and positive; life had been good to her. Her husband earned a fabulous income, and she was free to focus on their family, meticulously organizing every aspect of their lives, especially their social agenda.

Family meant everything in the world to her, and she wanted to instill those values in her children. She borrowed Sadie's recipes and learned to cook Michael's favorite ethnic foods in order to maintain his family's traditions. They celebrated both Christmas and Chanukah, displaying a Christmas tree and Menorah in their family room. The winter holidays were a big to-do. Lauren annually hosted both families at their home.

Lauren shopped and lunched with Toby at least once a week and often shared dinner with her or Michael's parents when he was away on business. Her background in education afforded her the patience to help Abbey with her schoolwork and solve any problems that gave her trouble. Lauren even got involved with the Home and School Association, raising money for the school to acquire the amenities it couldn't afford. She'd also accompany Abbey on school field trips to museums and the zoo; Lauren and Toby were always the first mothers to volunteer.

Despite Michael's frequent absences, Lauren was content with her life.

Michael often called home at dinnertime, and Abbey would always sprint to answer the ringing phone.

"Hi Abbey. How's my little girl doing?"

"Hi, Daddy."

"Are you being a good girl for Mommy?"

"Yep. Are you going to bring something home for me?"

"If you stay a good girl, Daddy will bring you a surprise."

"Okay, here's Mommy." Abbey dropped the phone.

"Hi honey. How's it coming along?" asked Lauren.

"I should be home by Thursday evening. Hopefully everything will work out."

"We miss you. Come back already."

"It's my top priority. By the way, I'm gonna hit some golf balls at the driving range over the weekend. I have a company golf outing next week and I need to work on my game."

"Okay," she reluctantly agreed.

"Alright, I'll see you when I get home. I have to meet a client for dinner shortly."

"Bye, I love you."

"Love you too."

———————————————————————

Chapter 17

aving just returned from his business trip, Michael was swamped at work. Nevertheless, his sights were set on the golf outing; he felt like he deserved a break from the daily chaos. In previous years, Michael had savored every waking minute of the retreat. He'd have the opportunity to catch up with some of his old work buddies, namely Jerry.

They tried to maintain their close relationship, but it had become more difficult now that they worked in different divisions and on separate floors of the building. Plus, Michael spent half of his time on the road, while Jerry stayed put in New York and worked the phones.

"Jerry's on the line for you," Michael's secretary announced. She transferred the call, and Michael put the phone to his ear.

"Hey Jerry! How've you been?"

"I'm doing fine. I just want to make sure you'll be out on the greens this weekend. I never know where in the world you are these days."

"I'll be there, alright."

"Great! I'll put together a foursome. Maybe Jonathon will join us."

"That'd be nice," Michael said. "Unexpected—but nice."

"While we're at it, let's break bread sometime this week."

"My schedule is a little tight, but I'll do my best," Michael promised.

"By the way, did you ever sell your position in GE? Remember that purchase from a few years back?"

"Hell yeah, I made fifty K on that sucker. Tell your buddy McGuire I owe him one," Michael said. "What did you do? Did you ever sell?"

"I wound up with a hundred-grand profit on the deal. What a payday! Get me a couple more of those tips, Mike, and we'll both be sitting at the pool nursing martinis instead of sucking down coffee at this dump." They both laughed. "See you on the golf course, then."

"Sure thing. Don't forget my six stroke handicap," Michael joked.

"I will, but make sure you bring your own pencil. Mine might not be capable of subtracting that large a number."

That year, the company golf outing was held at one of the most exclusive country clubs on Long Island. With cigars dangling from their mouths, Michael, Jerry, Bob, and Jonathon tackled the rolling green fairways.

Jonathon had come for a good round of golf, but he also planned to seize the opportunity to discuss some business with Michael and Bob. After all, he did sink a boatload of corporate money into their division. As they lugged their golf bags across the course, Jonathon picked Michael's brain.

"Hey Mike, how's everything coming along in Mergers?"

"It's going well. All of my hard work is starting to pay off."

"Where do you see yourself in the next couple of years?"

"Hopefully hiring more salespeople for our division to keep up with its exponential growth."

"That's great. I think we should start on that right now. We've created a significant buzz in the marketplace. Can't give our competition the opportunity to get ahead of the game. I'm gonna talk to the personnel department about it first thing Monday morning."

The foursome continued walking down the fairway, bags at their sides, until they reached the tee at the eighteenth hole. Jonathon stepped up to take his shot. He ripped off a powerful drive, sending the ball straight at the pin. It took a few bounces and rolled downhill, finally settling two feet from the green.

Jerry was up next. His shot landed a little to the right of the green, near some trees lining the fairway. Bob placed his ball on the tee and took his stance. He had the least golfing experience of the group, but he managed to drive the ball just as well. His shot landed right next to Jonathon's. The rest of the group stared in utter amazement.

Finally, it was Michael's turn. He placed the ball on the tee, studied it for a moment, and took a huge swing. The ball curved left and plopped right into a sand trap. Michael fiercely threw his club to the ground. "Damn it," he shouted. "Son of a—"

Chapter 18

The following week, Michael got a call from his old friend, Andrew Fox, with whom he hadn't spoken in a while. They both had crazy schedules; Andrew did just as much preparation for his cases as Michael did traveling. But they relished each other's company and always found time to relieve their stress over a meal, just like back in high school. To briefly forget their responsibilities for a few hours was a luxury for both.

Michael patiently waited for Andrew at their favorite watering hole, nursing a drink at the bar and checking his watch from time to time. Over the years, he'd come to accept his best friend's lack of punctuality.

"Hey Mike. How are you, pal?" Andrew asked, hurriedly approaching the bar.

"Long time no see," replied Michael, shaking his hand. "Let's get a table with a little more privacy. We've got a lot to catch up on." Michael settled up the bill with the bartender, and they moved to a table with less smoke and noise.

"How are Lauren and Abbey doing?"

"Aw, they're great. The little one just started ballet classes. Lauren's hoping she'll dance at the Academy of the Performing Arts someday."

"That'd be fantastic. Free front-row tickets!"

"Yeah, that would be nice. But we're not talking Titans or Yankees seats."

"Right. We can leave the wives and kids at home for those games. That's our time."

"Hear, hear," Michael declared, raising his glass. Andrew clinked his mug and took a healthy swig of beer.

"And here's also to happy, healthy times ahead."

"I can't believe how quickly Abbey's grown up. It feels like I brought her home from the hospital just yesterday."

"Yeah, well, you know what they say about time."

"What's that?" Michael jested.

"It fuckin' flies, buddy." They erupted in laughter.

Of all his high school pals, Michael had maintained a close relationship with only Andrew, who was gaining a reputation as one of Manhattan's most prominent criminal lawyers.

He started in the D.A.'s office fresh out of law school and quickly learned the ins and outs of the system. Since then, Andrew had opened his own defense practice, which represented clients accused of anything from petty theft to murder. Michael found his work to be incredibly fascinating.

"So how are things at the firm, Andy?"

"Busy. Very busy. I can barely keep up with all of my cases."

"Go on."

"You're not getting anything outta me, Mike. You know this stuff is confidential until it goes to trial."

"I know, I know. Can't blame me for trying, though."

"So does Lauren ever talk about going back into teaching?"

"She'll mention it every now and then, but I doubt it's in the cards. With the kid, our social agenda, and spending all of my hard-earned money at the department stores, she's pretty busy as it is."

Andrew nodded in recognition and sipped his drink.

"At least she's not sitting at home wondering when you'll be back for dinner. Seems like all my wife does lately is complain about how I'm not at home."

Andrew had fallen in love with his wife, Julie, while at college. She financially supported him through law school, and he felt indebted to her for his rising success.

"I know what you mean. Lauren's been bitchin' up a storm, too. We had parents' visitation at school a couple of weeks ago and, wouldn't you know it, something came up last minute and I had to shoot out of town. She was pissed."

They shared another laugh, realizing how much they still had in common.

"Have you and Julie talked about starting a family?" Michael pried.

"Oh, it's been discussed plenty. But she's still worried that I'll never be around to help out with the baby. You know how it is."

"That I do," Michael said.

"So, how about you? How's your new venture coming along?" Andrew asked.

"We're actually doing pretty well. My boss just gave me the go-ahead to hire more salespeople. The expansion should be exciting."

"I'm sure Lauren's looking forward to it," Andrew added.

"Yeah, right," Michael guffawed.

Andrew pulled a silver cigarette container from the inner pocket of his suit jacket and flipped it open for Michael, who politely declined. Nevertheless, he couldn't help but admire the tasteful monogram of Andrew's initials on the back of the case. They had sure come a long way since their days playing stickball in the streets of Brooklyn.

"Guess who I bumped into the other day?" Andrew asked.

"Who?"

"You'll never guess in a million years."

"Come on Andy, spill it,"

"Remember Alan?"

"Shit yeah. What's he up to these days?"

"I bumped into him in town last week. He gave me his business card." Andrew presented it to Michael.

"Bookkeeper. That's what he got into right after graduation, isn't it?'

"Oh yeah, you're right."

"How does he look?" Michael asked.

"A little heavier and balding. I didn't recognize him at first, but he singled me out of the crowd right away."

"You ever see anyone else from high school?" Michael inquired.

"No, not lately."

"What'll it be, fellas?" interrupted a throaty female voice.

A busty waitress stood beside the table, eager to take their order. Andrew couldn't take his eyes off her. Michael vaguely recognized this woman; the extra-short skirt that barely covered her ass sparked his memory. She had also flirted with him— there wasn't a chance he'd forget about that.

Last time he had just shrugged off her advances, but tonight he felt drawn to this waitress. Lost in his thoughts, Michael suddenly realized he was staring directly at her. He self-consciously turned in another direction, and she headed off towards the kitchen.

"Wow, that's some piece of ass," Andy noted.

"I've seen her before. Must've been three years ago, but I remember. That tight body—wow."

"She has her eye on you, Mike," he kidded. "Watch out!"

Michael parried the implication with a laugh, though he couldn't deny the spark he felt inside upon seeing her again.

"To tell you the truth, I do wonder what it'd be like to be single again," Michael admitted.

"No kidding. You've been with Lauren since high school. You probably can't even imagine what anyone else's touch would feel like."

"I remember my first," Michael snickered.

"Who was that? That cheerleader from sophomore year?"

"Oh, no. Not Rachel Rubin. I may not have even told you about this one."

"Yeah? Who was it?"

"Do you remember Babs?" Andrew froze in place, his beer mug nearly at his lips.

"Get outta here!"

"Swear to God. A few months after our little rendezvous in the closet, I called her up, walked over to her house, and popped her right there."

"You dog! I can't believe you held on to that one."

"Oh, come on. It was *Babs*, Andy."

They laughed the night away, polishing off multiple beers before calling for the check. Michael insisted on picking up the tab. He found a note stapled to the back of it, which read: "*Please call me anytime,*" with a phone number underneath. Michael discreetly concealed it in his pocket as he reached to retrieve his cash.

"It was good seeing you, Michael," Andrew said.

"Always a pleasure. We should do this more often."

They shook hands and set off in opposite directions. But Michael turned back to get one last look at that tantalizing waitress.

Chapter 19

Seasons passed, and Michael successfully enacted his game plan for the Mergers and Acquisitions division. A slew of new employees bustled through their offices on the 16th floor. M & A was the talk of Wall Street, no longer confined to the banking world. Major corporations started to gain the confidence of other institutions and subsequently employed Jones Bailey to raise capital for their ventures.

Michael's division had paved the way, building a successful sales force and increasing profits at an exponential rate. Michael brought home more money than his father could have ever imagined; his bonus checks were through the roof. Deals were struck left and right, and he received an override on every one of them. That ominous phone call from Jonathon Steinhardt had turned out to be a stroke of good fortune. Michael had certainly been at the right place at the right time.

Michael's life was changing, but in a positive way. His inflated salary enabled him to enjoy more and more luxuries, which included taking his family on vacations to exotic locations.

Their household celebrated another miracle in August of 1961. Lauren got pregnant and delivered another baby girl into the world. Ecstatic, they acquired the best baby furniture and clothes that money could buy for the newborn, whom they named Brittney.

Lauren began to shop at the higher end stores and even helped Michael pick out some expensive Hickey Freeman suits. Although the average household had only one car, the Aronsteins drove two. They also had their sights set on a new home. They were living well below their means; their tiny home in Oceanside was a far cry from what they could actually afford.

Michael had employed astute investment strategies to amass a diverse portfolio of stocks and bonds, in addition to a hefty pile of cash in a savings account. Their wishful thinking on the night of his proposal had become a reality.

Lauren contacted a realtor and looked at a number of different properties. She set her sights on a neighborhood in Kings Point on the north shore, not too far from Oceanside. Michael and Lauren had always talked about living by the water.

She eventually found her dream home, an old Tudor gated mansion with a magnificent view of the Long Island Sound. Lauren fell in love with it halfway through the initial tour and, a few days later, easily convinced Michael that it was the perfect home in which to raise their family.

Once he got a look at the backyard, with sailboats bobbing along the calm waters of the Sound, Michael became equally enamored with the property. Although it was a bit too pricy for their means, Michael's optimism won out. He was confident that his salary would continue to increase.

It was the spring of 1962, and the newly elected President John F. Kennedy had been in office for just about a year. Just as his cabinet worked to fulfill campaign promises, Michael strived to make good on his vow to provide for his family.

The moving van backed into their winding driveway early Monday morning. Michael had reluctantly stayed home from work to supervise the intricate operation. He was exhausted after spending the entire weekend packing up their tiny rancher.

As the children slept soundly on Sunday night, Michael and Lauren nearly pulled an all-nighter boxing their belongings. Their overwhelming excitement for the move dwarfed any thoughts of resting. They were starting a new leg in their lives and leaving fond memories behind.

The sun shone brightly on the morning of the big move, which Michael took as a sign of continued prosperity for him and his family.

"Ma'am, where would you like me to put this box?" asked one of the movers.

"Oh, just put it up in the master bedroom," Lauren said.

The furniture and boxes kept coming, and she directed the help like a drill sergeant commands his soldiers.

"Mommy, this is fun!" Abbey cried out, as she rode her tricycle in the center hall foyer.

"Which one is my room, Daddy?" asked Brittney, clutching her blankey and sucking her thumb.

"Hello, hello," rang out a shrill voice that was unmistakably Sadie Aronstein's.

Amidst all the commotion, Michael and Lauren had nearly forgotten that their parents were coming to help out with the move.

"Are you there?" Sadie called out. Becky and Herb were by her side.

"We're in here," Lauren shouted from the kitchen.

She removed glasses from a box and stored them in a cupboard above the upgraded kitchen appliances. These luxurious amenities, as well as the breakfast nook, had sparked Lauren's imagination when she first viewed the house. She envisioned all of the decadent meals she could prepare for her family.

"Mazel Tov, Mazel Tov, Mazel Tov!" Sadie said, embracing Lauren with a hug and kiss. "I don't know what else to say!"

"This is unbelievable," Herbie added.

"It's gorgeous," Becky gushed.

"What's in the bag?" asked Lauren, eyeing what Herbie set down on the table.

"Just some bread and salt. It's Jewish tradition to bring these foods into a new home. It's supposed to symbolize your fruitful future, in which you'll never go hungry," Sadie said.

"We also brought you a mezuzah to hang on the doorpost. It sanctifies your home and ensures that God will watch over it and keep the bad spirits away," Herbie explained.

"Oh, that's so thoughtful of you." Lauren hugged both of them again.

Michael, sweat pouring from his face, entered the room and greeted his parents. "Not too shabby for a little poor boy from Brooklyn," he touted.

"This is a dream come true," Herbie said.

"I feel like I'm in Cinderella's castle," Becky kidded.

"Come on, let me take you on a tour," Michael insisted.

"Is this the nickel or the ten cent tour?" joked Herbie.

"Can we come too, Daddy?" Brittney tugged on her father's pant leg.

Becky took each child by the hand, and they strolled through the first floor. Michael pointed out the library, family room, humungous living room, and equally large dining room, where they would hold holiday dinners in the future.

"Oh my God," Sadie uttered.

"This is unreal." Herbie shook his head in disbelief.

Michael slid open one of the patio doors and stepped out onto the porch. He implored them to sit down on the picnic bench and take in the gorgeous view of the lapping waters.

Brittney and Abbey were just as eager to show off their new digs. After admiring the view for a moment, they all returned inside and followed the girls up the spiral staircase to the bedrooms.

"This is my room," Abbey bragged.

"And this pink one is mine," Brittney said, pointing to an adjacent room that still smelled of fresh paint.

"And where will I sleep?" asked Herbie with a chuckle.

"These rooms are enormous," Sadie exclaimed.

The front door bell rang, and Michael excused himself to answer it. Victor and Martha Peterson greeted him at the door. Brittney and Abbey rushed to their father's side.

"This is beautiful," remarked Martha.

"I can't believe how big this place is," Victor said. He bent down to the children. "Give Grandpa a hug and kiss."

"Don't forget Grandma," added Martha.

"Hi Mom! Hi Dad!" Lauren yelled from the top of the stairs. She set aside the clothes she was unpacking and greeted her parents in the foyer. Martha presented a wrapped present, which she held under her arm.

"Mom, you shouldn't have done this. It's totally unnecessary."

"Oh, it's just a little sculpture of Christ. I think it would look great on the mantle over the fireplace you told me about. He'll watch over your home and bring good luck."

Lauren took her parents on another tour of the home while Michael and his folks sat in the breakfast area and enjoyed the view of the water. After which, they all congregated by the kitchen table to shoot the breeze.

Michael suggested that they check out the rest of the grounds. He led them around the perimeter of the property, proudly showing off the three-car garage and the two expensive vehicles inside.

"The former owner stored a little sailboat in here. He used to take it out on the water."

"Really? Must have been quite the big shot living here," Victor presumed.

"Actually, we heard it was a distant cousin of the Rockefellers." Michael boasted.

Later that night, after everyone had left, Michael removed the statue of Jesus Christ that was affixed on the mantle. Passing through the den, Lauren noticed its disappearance almost immediately.

"Michael, what happened to that Jesus piece my parents just gave us? I thought I placed it right up here."

"Oh, yeah, I put it away. There's no reason to leave it there. It's too blatantly religious; my family will be offended when they come and visit."

"Well that's not fair. Suppose I throw away the mezuzah you're planning to put up on the doorframe?"

"That's different. It's an ornament on the outside of the house. Most people wouldn't even know what it stands for. Besides, you wouldn't be forced to stare at it all day long."

"Oh, I'm sorry. I didn't know my religion was so offensive to you," Lauren snapped back.

Michael's ears reddened, and he moved towards the mantle. Brittney and Abbey crept down the stairs to sneak a glance at the brewing argument. They watched their father grab the statue and swing it up in the air like he was planning to smash it on the ground. But Michael held onto it and continued shouting at at his wife.

"This isn't a discussion, Lauren!" he screamed. Nearly bursting into tears, Lauren spied the girls out of the corner of her eye. They both bit their lips, their knees trembling. Lauren softened and turned away from Michael.

"It's okay, girls. Daddy's just a little upset. Go back upstairs." The girls scampered back to their rooms as they were told.

Michael remained by the mantle, frozen with the statue in his hand. He softly placed it back down on the wooden surface as Lauren stormed off to deal with the children.

Chapter 20

*D*espite the burgeoning difficulties with his marriage, Michael's business continued to flourish as a result of his hard work and some good fortune. Promoted to President of his division, Michael received a hefty bump in his salary, not that he needed it. He already showered Lauren with expensive jewelry on each birthday, anniversary, and other special occasions. Money was no object when it came to pleasing his wife. Plus, she adored those sparkling pieces.

Within the next year, Lauren gave birth to another little baby girl, whom they named Julia. Raising a family of three soon became overwhelming, so they hired a live-in nanny, a pleasant Jamaican-born woman named Mia. Since the children adored her, Michael and Lauren didn't hesitate to bring Mia along on family outings, and even some extended vacations.

Lauren and Michael joined an exclusive country club and rubbed elbows with some of the most affluent people in New York. The children attended elite private schools, where they received more personal attention, as well as dance classes and piano lessons on the baby grand in the living room. While Lauren devoted much of her time to the girls, going so far as to serve as den mother for the local girl scouts chapter, Michael became active in the synagogue. He was elected President of the men's club after securing a tremendous amount of donations for the temple.

Budding socialites, Michael and Lauren attended ballroom charity events and dinners and posed for pictures with the "who's who" of New York City. They developed a reputation throughout the community for their generosity. Despite coming from lesser means, they somehow learned how to blend right in with the elite.

With the help of an interior designer, Lauren furnished the entire household with an array of decorative pieces. Michael gradually forgot about the Jesus statue that remained atop the mantle, as it blended in with the surrounding pieces.

He focused on the exterior, arranging for the construction of tennis courts on some empty ground by the side of the house. These not only provided easy access to another form of recreation, but also gave him another venue at which to conduct business.

Although Michael made more money than he could ever imagine, he nevertheless perceived a giant void in his life. He had achieved so much at such a young age, it now seemed as if there weren't any more challenges left.

He needed to get himself out of these self-imposed doldrums. After all, he was intelligent, rich, and powerful. He struggled to understand why he still wasn't completely satisfied.

The demands of his position were extraordinary; he barely had enough time to spend with his family. Compounded with the stress of maintaining his prestigious lifestyle, keeping late hours and traveling the country to entertain clients had taken a toll on his body. Eventually, his and Lauren's relationship became strained; the imperfections of their union rose to the surface.

They had always disagreed as to which religion they would raise their children to practice. Michael wanted them to attend Hebrew Sunday schools, but Lauren wouldn't hear of it. He often flew off the handle, loudly voicing his frustrations when they argued. He could be stubborn, even arrogant at times, and was subject to frequent mood swings.

Despite his erratic temperament, Michael was consistently punctual, whether it was for a business meeting, golf outing, or simply a social appointment. On the other hand, Lauren was never on time—which drove him crazy. She habitually ran fifteen to twenty minutes late and left him waiting in the foyer, all ready to go.

That's where he found himself on the eve of the country club's annual Summer Lobster feast, the third of which Michael and Lauren would be attending.

"Let's go, dear. We're already going to be late!" he called upstairs.

"I told you. Just a few more minutes!" Lauren responded. She covered her eyes as she applied one last spritz of perfume. Standing before the full-length mirror, Lauren adjusted her outfit, which she had bought especially for this occasion. Satisfied with the healthy amount of cleavage that was exposed, she shut off the lights and went down to meet her husband.

Michael stood at the foot of the stairs, keys in hand, and tapped his Rolex in disapproval. Lauren's mermaid-shaped figure, which had always captivated him, now bulged at the hip. Along with her radiance, Lauren's vanity had disappeared into thin air. The burning flame between them was flickering out, in Michael's eyes, at least. But he kept such shallow thoughts to himself.

"You look gorgeous, honey. Glad to see that you made good use of the two hours it took to get ready."

"Oh, hush." She playfully slapped him on the arm and motioned to her figure as she twirled in place. "Rome wasn't built in a day," she purred, with a wink.

While Michael always had sex on his mind, his wife's suggestive behavior was a rare occurrence. She had come to view their lovemaking as more of a chore than a pleasurable experience since giving birth to three children. On occasion, she'd go for a quick roll in the hay, but otherwise Lauren remained focused on her children's lives. That wasn't nearly enough for Michael. His frustrations frequently bubbled to the surface in some other form.

Such tensions arose during the car ride over to the club. After a few minutes of silence, Michael voiced his concerns.

"I'm sorry to bring it up, Lauren, but this selfish behavior of yours has to stop."

"Selfish? I'm being selfish?"

"Yes, you are. I'm always ready at least twenty minutes before we're scheduled to leave, and you repeatedly make me wait nearly an hour. How do you think that feels?" Michael asked, somewhat rhetorically. Lauren exhaled a deep huff of frustration before she responded to the accusation.

"You've got some nerve, calling me selfish. I take care of the kids, day in and day out, so once in a while I like to spend a little time on myself—and for your benefit, too! Don't you want your wife to look good?"

"That's not the point," Michael started. He wanted to address her lack of interest in their sex life but trailed off as he realized his efforts would be in vain. They pulled up to the iron gates at the club's entrance and tacitly set the situation aside for the evening.

The valet took the keys to the sports car and sped off into the parking lot. Michael and Lauren entered the club and made their way into the cocktail lounge, where they parted ways. Michael headed towards some of his colleagues, and Lauren hightailed it over to a group of her girlfriends.

Shortly thereafter, the wait staff instructed the guests to make their way into the ballroom. Michael glanced over in Lauren's direction, but couldn't spot her amongst the gaggle of wives. He craned his neck and noticed that she was over in the corner of the room, engaged in conversation with a recently-divorced club member named Rodger. A little too engaged, in Michael's opinion. Lauren had a look in her eyes that Michael had scarcely seen as of late.

On the surface, Rodger didn't pose any threat to his marriage. Michael had done all he could for Lauren. He stayed fit, dressed in stylish attire, and ensured every last hair was in place before leaving the bathroom each morning.

If anything, Lauren ought to have been worried about losing him. Michael wasn't blind to the lascivious looks that various women shot him. Sometimes he couldn't tell if they were staring at his Rolex or his wedding ring, but he welcomed the attention anyhow. He'd proudly flaunt his expensive lifestyle to all who were interested.

Michael shuffled along with the crowd into the ballroom and took a seat at a table full of familiar faces. A moment later, Lauren and Rodger claimed the two remaining chairs. After the usual pleasantries were exchanged, a team of waiters emerged from the back kitchen with large trays stacked with fresh lobsters. Some were still twitching away the last moments of their lives.

Following the delectable lobster course, some casual conversation arose at the table. Lauren offhandedly complimented the gown that First Lady Jacqueline Kennedy wore on the cover of *Look* magazine, unintentionally sparking a heated discussion of racial issues and the politics involved.

Upon hearing the name "Kennedy," Rodger made an off-color joke that implied that the prominent family favored colored people. In any other situation, Michael would have let the derogatory remark slide by, but he felt the need to take Rodger down a notch. He piped up to staunchly defend the administration's efforts to bust up segregation in the South.

They went back and forth, with neither making any new points, and the volume of Michael's voice rose with each parry. Soon, the discussion was a full-on spectacle in the dining room. Embarrassed, Lauren kicked him underneath the table. He acknowledged her gesture, but shot her back a look that could choke a horse.

The entire table noticed Michael's rude response, but they didn't intervene. Lauren apologized to Rodger for her husband's behavior, and someone else quickly jumped in to steer the conversation in another direction.

Michael kept his thoughts to himself throughout the remainder of the meal and the awkwardly silent car ride home, but he finally exploded as soon as he and Lauren entered their bedroom.

"How dare you interrupt me when I'm talking to someone!" he shouted in a rage. He unloosened his tie and unbuttoned the top button of his collared shirt.

"You were making a total spectacle of yourself. Someone had to rescue you," she countered.

"Don't ever do that again!"

"Don't tell me what I can and can't do," she lashed back.

"I'll tell you one other thing you can't do—see anymore of that jerk Rodger. He's a pompous ass. And don't think I didn't notice how you were looking at him!"

"This is ridiculous. You're an ASSHOLE, Michael!"

That set him off. No longer able to control his violent temper, he pushed Lauren onto the bed and punched his fist through the wall.

"That's it! I've had enough!" he declared, storming out of the room.

"Where are you going?" she screamed.

"I need some fresh air. I'll be back," he shouted from the staircase.

"Mommy! Mommy! What's wrong?" cried out Abbey, who was awakened by the scuffle.

"Oh, it was nothing, honey. Just get back in bed. You have to get up early for school tomorrow, and it's very late."

Chapter 21

The argument pushed Michael to his breaking point. He had to blow off some steam, so he headed straight to his favorite watering hole in downtown Manhattan—where he felt at peace.

Upon entering the cocktail lounge, he sat down at a somewhat secluded table and scanned the bar to make sure nobody would recognize him and start asking questions. He had to be discreet this late at night. After a couple of minutes, a cocktail waitress approached his table. She looked familiar, but he couldn't quite place her. Then it dawned on him that she was the attractive seductress who had served him a few other times he'd stopped in.

"How are you, sweetie?" she purred. "What can I get for you?"

"Vodka on the rocks with a twist."

"Great, I'll be right back with that."

Michael's mind drifted back and forth between his confrontation at the country club and the dust-up with Lauren that followed. He convinced himself that leaving the house and letting things cool off was the right decision. But he couldn't help but fantasize about being single again. After all, Lauren was his high school sweetheart; he hadn't been with any other women since then.

Michael drowned his sorrows in liquor, ordering drink after drink as the evening wore on. By closing time, Michael was smashed. He was the last patron left in the bar, but he didn't care. At that moment, he didn't have a care in the world.

The waitress dropped off his check and sat down at Michael's table.

"What's your name?" she asked.

"I'm Michael. What's yours?"

"Maria."

"Did anybody ever tell you that you look like Elizabeth Taylor? A Hispanic version, though." he slurred.

"Oh, that's so sweet of you," she responded, clutching his hand. The touch of her warm skin aroused him—he could already sense an erection forming.

"Are you married?"

"I am. How about you?"

"Nope. Nothing that serious," Maria said with a smile.

"Do you live around here?"

"I live in the Bronx, not too far from the subway stop. You?"

"I live on the Island," said Michael.

"What are you doing all the way down here? No bars in your town?"

"I just wanted to be alone, and this is the perfect place. I'm usually here for lunch, since my office is close by." He glanced down at his watch. "Wow. Speaking of the office, I'd better get home. I have to be back here in a few hours."

Michael's legs wobbled as he rose from the table. He gripped the back of his chair to regain his balance.

"You can't drive this way," Maria advised. "Why don't you come to my place? I'll fix you a cup of coffee to sober you up a little bit. You could get into a serious accident or even kill someone."

Michael couldn't argue with her reasoning, so they shared a cab to her apartment.

"Come on in. Make yourself at home while I get you some coffee," she suggested, as she removed her jacket. Michael took a look around the apartment. He was amused by some of the decorative items—much more eclectic than those in his palace.

Maria carried on the conversation from the kitchen.

"I've lived in this neighborhood for years. Can't seem to leave it." She gently stirred the mug of instant coffee. "How would you like it?"

"Two sugars and a little milk or cream will do."

They made small talk as Michael sobered up. The coffee did the trick.

"I gotta go. It's getting late and I have to get back home."

"Hold on. Can you wait a minute?" He glanced at his watch and nodded.

It was already 2:00 AM. If he walked in this late, he could be in for another battle with Lauren, no matter his excuse.

Maria emerged from her bedroom, dressed in a shockingly revealing outfit and high-heeled shoes. Two red hearts covered her nipples, and her matching string panties had a heart concealing her crotch. In his vulnerable state, Michael was easily seduced.

It was the best sex he'd ever had--like nothing he could have imagined. After their passionate encounter, Michael got dressed and unknowingly dropped his wallet on her bedroom floor.

Michael returned home in the wee hours of the night, but his late arrival went undetected. Lauren was fast asleep when he came crashing in at 4:00 AM. He didn't sleep that night, knowing that he would have to wake up within the next two hours. He lied in bed and stared up at the ceiling, guilt ridden and remorseful, preparing himself to resume his normal routine the following morning. Like nothing had changed.

About an hour after lunch, the buzz of his intercom woke him—he'd dozed off in the middle of the workday.

"There's a Maria Salvatez on the phone for you. Would you like me to transfer it?" Caught off guard, he hesitated for a moment before realizing who was calling.

"Put her through," he said. He got up from his desk and quickly peeked out his office door to ensure that no one would overhear his conversation.

"Hello," he said with a hint of confusion.

"Hi Michael. Don't you remember me?"

"Of course, how could I forget?" he replied. "How did you get my number?"

"Don't worry. I'm just calling to let you know that you left your wallet in my apartment."

"Oh, jeez." He shook his head in total disbelief as he patted his pants pocket. "Well, how can I get it?"

"That's up to you," she responded in an enticing voice.

"Why don't you meet me at Jake's Steakhouse this evening? I'll treat you to dinner as a reward. It's the least I can do."

"What time?" He looked down at his watch.

"Around 6:00."

"I'll see you then," she said.

To cover his tracks, Michael told Lauren that a business meeting had been unexpectedly rescheduled. He said that he had to entertain an out-of-town client and that he'd be home late. She didn't question his alibi; she had long since accepted such disappointments as part of his job.

Michael sat at a secluded table as he waited for Maria to arrive. He stood up and waved his hand to get her attention once he spotted her talking to the maître d'. She acknowledged the gesture and approached his table.

Michael studied her body from a new, sober perspective. He couldn't repress the physical attraction. He was no longer thinking with his head. His penis had taken complete control.

"I'm so sorry to put you through this," she apologized.

"It's quite alright. Besides, it's my fault for leaving my wallet with such a pretty woman."

"Oh, that's so sweet of you," she said, affectionately clutching his hand.

As before, her touch sparked an uncontrollable sensation in his loins. They spoke about a variety of different subjects that evening, but she was particularly interested in his background.

Dinner finally concluded, and the waiter suggested the dessert menu.

"Why don't we pass on dessert, Michael? I have some delicious brownies at my place, and we can pick up some ice cream on the way."

He hesitated for a split-second but couldn't resist the temptation. They made it back to her apartment, one thing led to another, and they had passionate sex once again.

As Michael drove home that night, he couldn't get the tryst out of his mind. He was torn between his loyalty to his family and his paralyzing physical attraction to Maria. There was no turning back. There was another woman in his life, and he resolved to find a way to deal with the situation, rather than avoid it.

The following morning, as Lauren prepared breakfast, she asked, "How was your meeting, honey? You must have come home awfully late. I didn't even hear you come into bed."

She was attempting to put their heated argument from two nights before in the past. They hadn't spoken much since, and this small talk seemed like the perfect way to break the ice.

"The meeting went well. Sometimes these business dinners last longer than expected. You know that," he insisted with a straight face.

He didn't flinch. It came out naturally. He conducted his business in such a straightforward manner on a daily basis, so it wasn't difficult to bring it home to the kitchen table. Though he still felt uneasy about lying to his wife to cover his tracks.

He went over all the details in his mind, should Lauren press him any more on his whereabouts. But she still trusted him. That almost made it harder to lie to her. In her eyes, he hadn't done anything out of the ordinary. The thought of Michael cheating on her never entered Lauren's mind.

It was too late for him to go back. Michael had a taste of something new and didn't want to let it go. He couldn't get Maria out of his mind. He didn't plan for it to happen, but somehow it did.

Maria satisfied his sexual appetite in ways that Lauren never could. He still valued their marriage; the thought of just walking away never crossed his mind. He would never put his children through a divorce.

Chapter 22

*M*aria's long, silky black hair, bright green eyes, and flawless curves left him awestruck. At the young age of 24, her body was still tight as a drum. It was as though a sculptor molded every part to perfection. Her skin was as soft and radiant as a newborn baby's, without a hint of cellulite. She knew how to please him in bed, teaching him every new position under the sun and contorting her body in ways that Lauren could never dream of. Somehow this novel lovemaking distracted him from the guilt that still plagued his mind. He was addicted to her body; Maria catered to all of his wants and needs.

Michael carefully planned their meetings so as to avoid getting caught. With too much to lose if his tryst was exposed, he took every precaution not to disrupt his happy-go-lucky family life. He arranged dinner dates with Maria on occasional weeknights and treated her to meals at posh restaurants down in her neighborhood, where he wouldn't be recognized. Wild lovemaking always followed.

He now had a mistress by his side, the showpiece of his collection of expensive toys. Maria made him feel young again and bolstered his self-confidence. She was enthralled by his money and power, unlike Lauren, who, in Michael's opinion, took his hard work for granted.

Since things were going so well with Maria, Michael decided to do something a little different—more adventurous. He planned to whisk her away to Las Vegas for a quick three-day extravaganza in the middle of the week. They could see some shows, dine at the finest restaurants, and do a little bit of gambling.

He shut his office door, rested the heels of his shiny black shoes upon the desk, and picked up the phone.

"Maria, do you have a minute?"

"I was just running out the door, but I always have time for you, honey. What's up? Do you want to see me tonight?" she asked in her enticing voice.

"I would, but I have other plans that I can't break," he replied. "I called to see if you would join me on a trip to Vegas next week."

"Are you kidding?" She was flabbergasted.

"No, I really mean it."

"I would love to, Michael. Just tell me when, where, and how. I'll be there with bells on—or off, if you'd prefer," she giggled.

She caught a cab to the airport the following Tuesday morning, and Michael met her at the terminal with two roundtrip tickets. Thrilled to get away for a few days, she greeted him with open arms and a big smile. It almost seemed like they were setting off on their honeymoon.

Maria had heard so much about the glitz and glamour of Vegas and couldn't wait to see it for herself. She packed every sexy negligee she owned and fantasized about all of the ways she would make love to Michael once they were thousands of miles away from his family.

Michael told Lauren and the kids that he was going on a short business trip to Chicago and would return shortly. He had shopped for casual sportswear earlier in the week and conveniently stored it in a packed suitcase in his office, since such garments clearly weren't suitable for a business trip to Chicago in the dead of winter. If Lauren had spied the bathing suits and shorts while helping him pack, it would have raised some red flags.

To further disguise his trip, Michael booked a flight from New York to Chicago. He checked into a hotel by the Chicago airport so that he could call the front desk from Vegas to check his messages. He had to cover every base in the event that his wife or office tried to get in touch with him. No one would question that he was working in Chicago.

They arrived in Vegas and checked into the Stardust Hotel that afternoon. It was a beautiful sunny day, and the temperature reached 87 degrees, a far cry from the cold and blistery weather they had left in New York. The change of climate put them both in great spirits.

The bellhop escorted them to their custom suite, which contained a round bed and a mirror affixed on the ceiling above it.

Michael didn't miss a trick. He tipped the bellhop and immediately threw Maria onto the bed without even unpacking their luggage. He nibbled at her earlobes and unbuttoned her blouse, undressing her piece by piece. He licked every part of her body as though it were an ice cream cone—his favorite flavor. She squeezed her eyes shut, relishing every invigorating moment. He loosened his tie, and she unbuttoned his shirt, simultaneously dragging her tongue down his chest. They furiously made love, watching every move on the mirror that hung above as if it were a silver screen.

Afterwards, they lied by the pool and sipped exotic cocktails in the blazing sun. Michael insisted on sitting under an umbrella to read the *Wall Street Journal*. Even in Las Vegas, he attempted to disguise himself with a straw hat and dark sunglasses. He also made sure not to spend too much time in the sun; he couldn't afford to come home with a glowing tan. Maria laid on a chaise lounge beside him, soaking up the rays, the straps of her two-piece bathing suit hanging off her shoulders.

As the sun set, Maria rose from her chair and accidentally tripped on her high-heeled sandals. She landed right on her face and bruised her left eye.

"Are you alright?" Michael immediately ran to her aid. A group of fellow sunbathers dropped their reading material at the sound of the commotion.

"I'm just clumsy." She shrugged it off.

They decided to head back to the room to take showers and relax before dinner. Michael had made reservations at the most expensive restaurant in the hotel, where the comedian Jerry Lewis and singer Sammy Davis Jr. were performing that evening.

They were lying in bed together, killing time before the show, when Michael glanced at his watch and realized that it was already 8:30 PM back in New York. He had to call the front desk at the Chicago hotel to retrieve his messages.

The clerk told him that Lauren had left a message at approximately 4:30 PM Chicago time, which was right around dinnertime at the Aronstein household. All of his kids were likely congregated around the kitchen table waiting to talk to their father before starting their homework.

He asked Maria to shut off the TV and keep quiet so that there would be no distractions when he called back. He internally rehearsed his responses in case Lauren asked any detailed questions.

"Honey, is that you?" Lauren asked sweetly.

"Yes dear, it's me. I'm sorry I missed your call. I was out to dinner with a client and just got back to the room."

"The children already miss you and can't wait for you to come home. They wanted to talk to you, but now they're all fast asleep."

As he spoke with Lauren, Maria remained in bed with a towel wrapped around her head, gazing at her fingernails, gnashing on a wad of gum, and incessantly blowing bubbles that popped with loud smacking sounds. She took a peek at her toes to ensure that they looked just right, since she planned to wear an open-toed shoe with her dress that evening.

She pulled a pocket mirror from her purse to see if she had gotten any color that afternoon. To her dismay, a black and blue shiner sat right under her swollen eye. It looked like she'd been hit by a heavyweight champ. She panicked and screamed "Dios mio!" Michael put his finger to his mouth to silence her, but it was too late.

"What was that outburst, Michael?" Lauren asked.

"Oh, it was just something on television," he fibbed.

Maria's vanity had almost cost him everything in that short span of a few seconds. She couldn't have cared less about his conversation or the impact that such a slip-up could have on his marriage. It was his problem, not hers.

"Honey, when are you coming home?"

"Not for a couple more days. I have a big deal pending, and I need to meet with the big shots of this company to finalize it. You know how these things work."

"I spoke with your parents earlier, and they said they're hosting a birthday brunch for Becky on Sunday. Your mom wanted to make sure that we'd be there."

"Absolutely! I wouldn't miss it for the world." He paused. "Sorry hun, but I have to go now."

"Okay, I'll see you when you get home," she cheerfully responded. "Love ya."

"Love you too," he replied.

He hung up the phone and kissed Maria's bruised eye to soothe the pain. That just reopened the floodgates; he couldn't resist her. They made love again and then got dressed for dinner.

With her impossibly short skirt and high heels accentuating her pristinely shaped legs, Maria could turn the head of any man. They walked down the corridor and waited patiently for the elevator to arrive. Maria had concealed her eye with dark sunglasses, which added to her mystique.

The elevator doors opened, and a vaguely recognizable voice shouted, "Michael! Michael Aronstein! Is that you?" Michael studied the man's face for a second but didn't immediately make the connection.

"It's Freddie from high school, you old dog."

He reached out to shake Michael's hand and pulled him in for a hug. Michael barely recognized his old friend; Freddie had put on some weight and was nearly bald.

"How the heck have you been? You haven't changed since high school," Freddie said. "What are you doing in this neck of the woods?" Michael was at a loss for words.

"This is my wife, Ann," Freddie continued.

"This is Maria," Michael reciprocated, careful not to mention the nature of their relationship. As Maria tipped her head in acknowledgement, her sunglasses fell to the floor, exposing her black and blue eye. She quickly knelt down to retrieve the glasses, but Freddie spotted the bruise before she could replace them.

"Wow, how did you do that?" he asked.

"Oh, I just fell down by the pool. I can be clumsy sometimes." She didn't elaborate any further.

Uncomfortable, Michael hoped to end the conversation before Freddie could ask any more questions. The elevator doors opened, revealing the casino floor. Michael exited at a rapid pace to shake Freddie loose, but his happy-go-lucky pal kept up and continued the conversation. He wouldn't let go.

"I moved out here several years ago to be with my family. Are you still in New York?"

"Yeah," Michael said, walking even faster.

"Do you see anyone from the old high school gang?"

"Not really." Michael gave curt responses, hoping Freddie would get the message.

"Why don't you write down your phone number so we can catch up?" Freddie suggested.

"I would, but I'm in kind of a hurry. We're running late for a show. I'll call your room later tonight." With that, he took Maria's hand and whisked her away.

"There's something strange about that Michael," Freddie whispered to his wife, as they watched him and Maria scamper off.

A tad shaken by the encounter, Michael escorted Maria into the restaurant. He gave his name and casually slipped the maitre'd a twenty-dollar bill. With a smile, the host led them to a cozy booth right in front of the stage.

They ordered their entrees—Maria got the most expensive thing on the menu—and sipped on glasses of wine. For some reason, Maria wasn't as chatty as usual.

"What's wrong, babe?" Michael asked.

"It's nothing."

"No, come on. Tell me."

"It's just—" She set down her fork and swallowed the last remnant of food still in her mouth. "Even here, we have to sneak around. First with your wife and then with that guy you ran into. When will it end?"

"You were fully aware of my situation when we started this whole thing," Michael protested.

"This whole thing—what is this, anyway? Do you enjoy my company? Or is it just the sex?" Her volume increased as she placed emphasis on the last word. Michael whirled his head around to make sure no one caught her outburst.

"I care about you a lot, Maria. I wouldn't be here with you if I didn't. Of course it's more than just sex. That's a silly question."

"Well I'm tired of playing second fiddle to Lauren. I'm in love with you, baby. I know it wasn't supposed to happen, but I can't help myself."

Michael nearly choked on a piece of steak. He coughed a few times and wiped his mouth with a cloth napkin.

"I'm not sure what to say. I'm flattered. And I have strong feelings for you, but—I'm married, to the mother of my children. I can't leave them." Maria's face fell.

"So you don't see any future for us?"

"That's not what I said. I want everything to stay like it is for now. We'll see about the future when it comes."

Maria was disappointed, but couldn't complain too much. After all, she was front row center for Jerry Lewis and Sammy Davis, Jr. in Las Vegas. It was the hottest ticket on the strip.

After the show, Maria and Michael strolled into the casino and tried their luck pulling the one-armed bandits until she got tired. They made their way back to their suite, where Maria fell asleep almost as soon as her head touched the pillow. Michael lied awake, tossing and turning, unable to find a comfortable position.

Careful not to wake Maria, he slowly crept out of bed, got dressed, and tiptoed out of the room. He put his hat and sunglasses back on, headed back to the casino, and sat down at a high-stakes blackjack table. The shoe must have been hot, because he amassed a stack of chips the height of the Eiffel Tower.

One by one, onlookers stopped to watch his lucky streak. The sexy cocktail waitresses kept bringing him drinks, and he continued to gulp them down. As he slowly became intoxicated, Michael let his guard down, absentmindedly removing his hat and shades.

He became abrasive and obnoxiously loud. His mound of winnings attracted two sexy hookers, who stood behind him making conversation, hoping they too could cash in. He welcomed their attention, as he was captured by their incredible bodies, and conversed with them in between hands.

Suddenly a camera flash illuminated the floor, embedding the image of Michael and the prostitutes in a photographer's camera. Michael looked up, and there was another flash. Unbeknownst to Michael, his old pal Freddie had taken the shots.

Michael panicked, and left the table after quickly gathering all of his chips. Instinctively, he headed straight for the cage to cash out his winnings. He brushed the incident off and went back to his room.

As their Las Vegas extravaganza continued, Michael showered Maria with lavish gifts, dinners, and shows, while she repaid him with unimaginable sex throughout their mini-vacation.

Chapter 23

7he plane touched down on the tarmac in New York late Thursday night. It taxied to gate B1, and the passengers deplaned into the TWA terminal. Michael kissed Maria goodbye and put her in a cab.

He drove through the security gates that surrounded his fortress, which was dimly lit by a series of lampposts. After pulling into the garage, he removed his decoy suitcase from the trunk, leaving the other bag. He intended to wash its contents at Maria's apartment. Then he realized that the wrinkle-free clothes in his decoy suitcase would arouse suspicion. He tiptoed into the laundry room attached to the garage and dumped the neatly folded clothes into the washing machine, then returned to the foyer, where he spotted a dish of cookies resting on a credenza. The note at its side read:

Dear Daddy:

We baked these cookies especially for you. We hope that you enjoy them and they make you happy after a hard day's work.

Love,
Julia, Abbey, and Brittney

Michael was touched, but a sense of guilt still pervaded. He pitter-pattered up the steps and entered each girl's room, kissing their foreheads as they slept. It relieved some of the self-inflicted pain he felt. He undressed and quietly rolled into bed so as not to disturb Lauren's slumber. Still in a deep sleep, she turned and moaned, "Hi honey."

He lied there, wide awake, staring at the ceiling and thinking about how he'd find a way out of the mess he had gotten himself into. He'd let himself get in too deep with Maria, and she knew more about him than he would have liked. How would their relationship play out in the end? Was it all worth it?

On the one hand, the void in his life vanished once Maria entered the picture; he was happier than he'd been in years. Yet he felt torn between the adoration of his loving family and the sexual gratification he received from Maria. He didn't want to upset the apple cart.

Michael alleviated his guilt and compensated for his misdeeds by surprising his children with expensive toys and Lauren with some more lavish jewelry. Breaking up his marriage never crossed his mind; it'd be much too painful for his children. He wouldn't be able to deal with the repercussions either.

Besides, his and Maria's relationship was consensual. Each of them had their own selfish reasons for continuing the affair. She didn't come right out and ask him to leave Lauren. She was content with the fancy restaurants, occasional vacations, and gifts that Michael provided. It was a no-strings-attached arrangement.

Michael's bond with his children remained strong, and his marriage was intact. His career flourished, and he made the front page of the Wall Street Journal from time to time. The publication praised his orchestration of multi-million dollar deals at such a young age, further boosting his already inflated ego.

As months passed, Michael couldn't force himself to part with Maria—and the sexual gratification. His life became even more complicated as he juggled work, family, and a full-on mistress. He needed to defuse some of those pressures, so he presented Maria with the idea of moving her out of her old-fashioned apartment in the Bronx to something more lavish in Manhattan, closer to his office.

She entertained the thought, but only agreed provided that she could decorate the apartment with new, expensive furniture. He caved to her whims and told her to let her imagination run wild. Michael didn't mind the extra expense, since it would benefit him in the long run. She'd be much closer to his office and removed from her current crime-infested neighborhood.

Maria started apartment hunting with a realtor and fell in love with the last one they toured. Upon leaving, she resolved to take Michael back to see it. Maria was confident that he'd approve; the place was magnificent.

Two days later, Michael was tidying up his office before leaving to meet Maria and the realtor for their scheduled appointment. Just as he started to walk out the door, the phone rang. It was Lauren on the other end.

"Is that you honey?" she asked.

"Yes it's me," he cringed.

"Is everything okay?"

"Yeah, what's up?"

"Don't forget to bring home the flowers for Julia's dance recital tonight."

"What recital?"

"You know, the one we spoke of last week at dinner."

"Aww, son-of-a-!" With so many things weighing on his mind, he had simply forgotten to put it on his calendar, as he always did with all important events. He now had to conjure up another story to cover his tracks.

"Honey, I told you I had a dinner meeting with a client this evening," he lied.

"The kids will be so disappointed if you don't show up."

"I can't get out of this one, but I'll try my best to brake it early" he sighed, wanting to appease her.

"Just give me the address of the school. I'll have our company florist deliver a dozen roses, no matter the cost. They're still open," he insisted.

She hung up the phone, disappointed that she'd have to fend for herself another night.

Michael couldn't believe what he had just done. Inside he knew that allowing Maria to take precedence over his family was unconscionable, but in the face of pressure he had somehow rationalized the decision. This better be a fucking stunning apartment, he thought to himself.

Chapter 24

Two years had passed since Maria moved into her midtown Manhattan apartment at Madison Terrace. During that time, she used Michael's money to furnish it in exquisite taste. Michael made good use of his second "home" and had fallen into a comfort zone.

Maria never called him, but instead waited for him to reach out. Michael had adamantly insisted on that arrangement from the get-go, demanding full control of the relationship. He was a control freak, just as he was in business.

One ordinary Tuesday, Michael and Robert Jorgensen were discussing the details of a big deal in the pipeline, when Michael's secretary interrupted.

"Michael, there's a Maria for you on line two," she announced.

"Tell her to hold on a minute." He was taken aback, but he knew he had to take the call, in case it was an emergency.

"Bob, you're going to have to excuse me for a minute. In the meantime, why don't you pull the IBM file?"

He shut the door behind Bob and answered the phone, gritting his teeth.

"Maria, I told you never to call me. What's wrong?"

"I don't know how to tell you this, but I'm pregnant."

"You're what?"

"I said—I'm pregnant!"

"That can't be."

"It's true. I'm three months gone."

"Impossible. I thought you were on the pill. How could this happen?"

"I never told you, but my doctor recommended that I get off the pill for a little while because I was having some sort of an allergic reaction. He told me to stop until he could determine what was causing the rashes."

"And now you tell me?" he snapped.

"Well, the baby is yours."

"Listen, I'm too goddamned busy to talk about this right now. Can it wait until I get to your place tonight?"

"Michael, I have to work."

"I'll meet you at the restaurant."

"Okay," she reluctantly agreed.

Michael was deeply perplexed. His smooth operation had been derailed. He wasn't prepared to deal with such a bombshell. Furthermore, he had to conjure up another excuse to get out of his plans with Lauren and the kids for the evening. He hated to disappoint them, but Maria's condition took precedence.

At the end of the day, he quickly tidied up his office, packed his briefcase, and stared out his window at the dark gray clouds that hung in the sky. Interim flashes of lightning and sounds of thunder clashed like two titans. It looked as though the gates of heaven were opening up.

Michael took his trench coat and umbrella from the stand behind his desk and waved down a cab outside the building.

Maria wasn't at the cocktail lounge when he arrived. Her co-worker Angelina told him that she had called in sick. He quickly hailed another cab and went to her apartment.

Even though the security guard, Lucian, extended a familiar greeting, he insisted that Michael sign the guest registry. Lucian always adhered to the building's strict policies, and Michael was technically a guest of Maria's.

Michael patiently waited for the elevator doors to open, then pushed the button for her floor upon entering. He soared up eleven flights and sprinted down the familiar corridor. Before he could press the doorbell on the center of her door, Maria swung it open. He stormed in.

"Hi baby," she cooed, lunging at him. She was excited to see him, as she hoped that the child growing inside her would cement the close bond between them, regardless of the nebulous nature of their relationship.

He pulled back, extinguishing her enthusiasm.

"Why didn't you tell me that you weren't going to work? I just came from the bar!"

"You said not to call you, didn't you?"

"You can't keep the baby," he demanded, moving onto more serious matters.

"Michael, I want this child. I want to be able to wake up every day and see a part of you there. Please—we have something special, and now no one will ever be able to take that away from us. This is a gift that we can share for the rest of our lives."

She moved closer to him, rubbing his chest, trying to change his mind. She had a knack for using her sexuality to manipulate him. He pushed her away.

"This is totally ludicrous," he said, coming to his senses. "You have to give it up. I'll cover all of the medical bills. You won't have to worry about a thing."

"No, Michael." She was firm in her convictions. He tried to reason with her.

"Maria, this can't go on. My career, my marriage, my children, everything that I've worked so hard for could go up in smoke if this ever gets out."

"Well you should have thought about that before you started fucking me!" Anger lit up her eyes.

"I'll deny it. It's your word against mine. Besides, they'll think you're some sort of a sleazy hooker trying to extort money from an innocent, law-abiding citizen. It's over, Maria. I'm out of here."

"I'll call your wife and tell her what you're really made of!"

He slapped her. She instinctively attacked him. They struggled. She clawed his face with her long nails, leaving deep marks embedded in his skin. In defense, he grasped both of her wrists and squeezed them until her hands turned a deep red.

Once she had relented, Michael let go. Maria grabbed her stomach, instinctively protecting the unborn baby. She fell onto the couch and lied there motionless, yet still breathing. Michael feared that he had taken it too far, but he didn't see any blood. He had barely touched her. This was just an act, a ploy to gain his sympathy.

In a panic, he hastily darted from the apartment, forgetting his umbrella in the hurry. As he paced down the hallway, most likely for the last time, Michael felt a sense of relief come over him. He wouldn't have to sneak around anymore. It was all over between him and Maria.

Even so, he couldn't return home with scratch marks all over his face. As the taxi passed a drug store, Michael signaled for the driver to stop.

He rushed inside and asked the cashier where to find the concealer. Michael gestured to the scratches on his face to further clarify what he was looking for, and then followed the employee down the makeup aisle. Michael was thankful that she didn't ask any questions.

Chapter 25

*M*ichael didn't contact Maria over the next few days. He never wanted to see her again. In fact, he wished he could erase his memory of her existence. Now, more than ever, he wanted to be the model father and husband that his family deserved.

At his company's monthly corporate meeting that Wednesday afternoon, Michael sat among his fellow divisional presidents. As usual, he was the youngest one. Water pitchers, fruit bowls, and silver coffee decanters were positioned at the center of the conference table.

With their pads and pens neatly placed before them, the executives were prepared to discuss the company's operations and their new strategies for moving forward. All eyes were set on Jonathon Steinhardt, who sat at the head of the large oval table.

The meeting came to order.

"I am pleased to announce that we're still headed in the right direction," Jonathon proclaimed. "Our profits have skyrocketed since last quarter."

Applause resonated from the executives.

"We are up almost twenty-five percent, thanks largely to Mergers & Acquisitions. Michael, stand up and tell us what's going on," Jonathon directed.

As Michael stood to address his colleagues, Jonathon's secretary rushed to his side and whispered something in his ear. Jonathon just nodded, processed the new information, and then interrupted the proceedings.

"Excuse me, Michael, somebody has to speak with you out in the corridor. It's a very important matter—so you can fill us in later on."

Michael excused himself, puzzled as to what could be so urgent. The first thoughts that entered his mind were that Maria showed up in a rage, or, God forbid, that a family member was in trouble.

Out in the hallway, two individuals dressed in suits greeted him.

"Are you Michael Aronstein?" asked the one with red hair. Flashing a silver badge, he introduced himself as Detective Timothy Fitzgerald and his partner as Christopher O'Rourke.

"Why are you here? What's wrong?" Michael asked, trembling.

"We'd like to talk to you about Maria Salvatez."

"What about her?"

"She was found dead last night in her apartment."

Michael face curled up in total shock. Even though he didn't kill her, he sensed that he could be in serious trouble. At the very least, his affair would be exposed and his marriage ruined.

"So what does that have to do with me?" Michael sputtered.

"You were the last one seen entering her apartment."

"So? That doesn't make me a killer," he pleaded.

"How about we go somewhere else to discuss this in further detail?" asked Detective Fitzgerald.

"Sure, let's go to my office."

"No, I think we'd be more comfortable downtown," Detective O'Rourke insisted.

"Can't we do this later on today? I'm in the middle of a meeting," Michael pleaded.

"I'm sorry, Mr. Aronstein, but we have to leave now," instructed Fitzgerald.

"At least let me tell my secretary where I'm going."

"Now!" he ordered, in a powerful voice.

The detectives escorted Michael out of the building and into an awaiting unmarked police vehicle. Upon entering the station, he was led to a small, windowless room for a proper interrogation.

They read him his rights, and Michael elected to summon his attorney, Andrew Fox, before proceeding. His thoughts were churning; a scandal could ruin everything.

An hour later, Andrew entered and cried out, "What the hell is going on here?" He was shocked to find Michael, who was usually so composed and cocksure, in such a distraught state, much less under arrest for murder.

"Andy, I didn't do it," Michael began.

"Then what the hell's this all about?"

"It's—not so simple."

"Why don't you tell me the truth so I can help you," he pleaded.

"I've been cheating on Lauren."

"You what?"

"I've been seeing this woman, Maria, for a while. God, it's been years." Michael let that hang in the air before continuing, "Last night, she was murdered. And they're trying to pin it on me."

"I don't understand. How could you—"

"I know I messed up, but I swear I didn't kill her, Andy!"

"Let's start from the very beginning."

"I went to her apartment last night, and we had an argument, which turned into a little scuffle. Nothing major, I just had to fight her off of me. When I stormed out, she was lying on the sofa, and that was the last time I saw her. She was very much alive, I swear. I didn't do this." He began to cry.

"I believe you, Michael. But does Lauren have any idea what's going on?"

"No, I haven't told her yet," he blubbered.

"Well, she's going to find out sooner or later."

Lauren was at Julia's private school for parent-student day. They were having a great time until an aide pulled Lauren aside to take a phone call in the front office.

"Where are you going, Mommy?" Julia asked.

"I'll be back in a minute," she assured her daughter.

Lauren hurried into the office and picked up the phone. A familiar voice was on the other end.

"Lauren?"

"Yes. What's the matter, Andrew?"

"It's Michael."

"Is he alright?"

"Not really."

"What's the problem?" A bit of panic set in.

"You'd better get down here."

"Where? Where are you, Andrew? What's going on?"

"I'm at the main police station in downtown Manhattan. I don't think you want to hear this over the phone."

A sergeant escorted Lauren to the holding room, where Michael sat with Andrew. Frantically crying, she embraced her husband.

"Are you alright, Michael? This must be some sort of mistake," she cried out. "What is this all about honey?"

Michael's emotions got the best of him. Tears streamed from his eyes.

"I don't know how to tell you this, but I've been unfaithful." Lauren's compassion instantly transformed to anger.

"What do you mean?" she shouted. "What does that have to do with you being here, under arrest?"

"The girl that I'd been seeing was murdered, and—and I'm their primary suspect."

"Oh my God! How could you do this?" Lauren stormed out of the room and slammed the door behind her.

Later that day, after Michael was booked and processed, a camera snapped a mugshot of his face, which had once lit up the front page of the Wall Street Journal.

All hell broke loose as soon as the press got wind of the story. Michael's face was plastered on the front page of every newspaper in town. Local television networks broadcasted from the front of his sprawling mansion. Michael had made the headlines again, but this time it wasn't a triumph.

Every reporter tried to get a glimpse of his family and a word with Lauren, the other victim in the whole debacle. Understandably, she was angry, humiliated, traumatized, and frustrated all at the same time.

"I can't believe that he could do such a thing!" Lauren exclaimed, tightly clutching a tissue after arriving home from the police station. "That bastard! How could he do this to us? Where was his head? Did he really think that he could get away with this?" She paused for a moment, thinking over the question.

"Now that I think about it, he came home the other night with scratches all over his face. He said it was from a dull razor. Oh God, maybe he did kill her," she whimpered.

Lauren's mother comforted her as she cried hysterically. Andrew stood nearby, reviewing some legal documents pertaining to Michael's case. More than just his lawyer, Andrew pledged to do everything he could to help Michael's family while the case played itself out.

"It'll be alright," Andrew assured Lauren. "He didn't do it. Michael swore up and down that the only crime he committed was having an affair. He didn't want it to come out this way. He just wants to wake up from this nightmare. Trust me, I will get to the bottom of this. Michael is many things, but he's not a murderer." That seemed to ease Lauren's suffering for a spell.

"What are the next steps?" she sputtered.

"He'll be arraigned before a judge. Even if they find sufficient evidence to hold him, he can always post bail."

"You can tell him to pack his belongings and live someplace else. I don't ever want to see or hear from him again."

"Lauren, don't you think that's a rash decision? You're not thinking clearly right now. Maybe the two of you can work this out."

"There is nothing to work out!"

Suddenly, sounds of shuffling feet came from the spiral staircase.

Julia shouted, "Mommy! Mommy! I just saw Daddy on television."

Lauren could no longer shelter her children from truth. The earth-shattering truth. All of their friends and neighbors would eventually find out, too. Her misery would be the topic of every conversation.

Andrew made his exit through the tightly secured gates and reached the huge amorphous crowd of news media standing outside.

"Mr. Fox," they shouted, "Did Michael do it? Why did he do it?"

Andrew stopped and rolled down his window. "My client did not kill Maria Salvatez. He will be cleared of all charges. That is all." And he sped off.

Chapter 26

The next morning, before his scheduled arraignment, Michael met with Andrew in one of the station's many empty interrogation rooms. His old friend and now his lawyer, Andy did his best to approach the situation delicately, as he would have with any client.

"Listen, Mike—" Andrew picked up his yellow legal pad and pulled a pen from his shirt pocket. "I want you to start from the beginning. Don't hold anything back just because I'm the one asking the questions. I won't pass any judgment, I promise. But I need the facts before I can let you go up there and enter a 'not guilty' plea."

Michael exhaled deeply and straightened himself in the metal chair, though there was no use trying to get comfortable in city-issued furniture.

"Thanks. Go ahead, then, ask away."

Andrew began, "Alright. When did you first meet Maria?"

"Years ago. She waited on me—actually I think you were there too—at the joint down the street from my office."

"Okay. And when did you start—you know, your affair?" Andrew coughed out the last word, seemingly unable to move beyond anything more graphic than a euphemism.

"Not until almost a year later. Lauren and I were fighting, so I just thought—"

Michael choked up, his voice dropping into a hoarse whisper. Everything would be out on the table. All at once, the shame and utter embarrassment of his indiscretions whacked him square in the face.

His children would find out the truth sooner or later, if they hadn't already. The last time he'd seen Lauren, she was storming out of the police station, causing any officers in her path to step aside with trepidation. She wasn't the first wronged spouse to barrel down that hallway.

Michael went on to detail for Andrew the circumstances of his and Maria's first sexual encounter and the subsequent progression of their relationship. As he retraced the trail of lies, deception, and sexual indiscretions, Michael perceived a slight jolt in his veins. A wave of blood rushed to his head, morphing into a warm sensation that gently spread through his body like a runny egg over toast.

The immense stress loosened the stranglehold on his brain. For the first time since his arrest, Michael thought of poor Maria. They really did have something together.

Andrew flipped through the nine pages of notes he had down on his pad. "So far all I have down here is the outline for some kind of depraved romance novel. Let's get to the crime. Where were you the other night? The night of—" he trailed off.

"After work, I took a cab to the bar to meet Maria, but she wasn't there. She had called out sick. It was miserable outside, pouring rain, so I was pretty pissed off that she had me running around town."

"How pissed?" Andrew croaked.

"Not *that* pissed, man. Come on. I know I'm far from innocent in this whole thing—I was unfaithful to Lauren—but

I didn't kill Maria! I could never kill anyone! You know that, right?"

"Yes, of course. I simply wanted—you know what, forget it. Keep going."

"So I hopped in a cab to Maria's place and gave her a piece of my mind. She screamed back at me, and I slapped her—just once, and not too hard. Then she started clawing at my face, so I took her by the arms, like this," Michael reached over the table and clasped Andrew by the wrists.

"And shoved her back against the wall. Just to calm her down, you know. No punching or choking--nothing serious like that."

Andrew nodded in understanding. "Okay."

"Then I stormed out. So quickly that I forgot my umbrella. I went downstairs, hailed another cab, and stopped at a drug store for some concealer."

Andrew gave him a puzzled look.

"To cover up the scratches. See?" Michael moved his face closer to Andrew's. The gouges had begun to heal, but were still visible.

"No, tell me again where you left Maria."

"She was on the sofa," Michael repeated. Andrew paged through his notes, searching for photos from the crime scene.

"There it is." He pulled a sheet from his file and presented it to Michael. Maria's bedroom—pairs of her underwear were strewn all over the floor. The formation of the miniature plastic markers, which were arranged by the officer on the scene, indicated that her nude body was found on the floor of her bedroom.

"You see? I couldn't have done this. Last I saw Maria, she was on the sofa in her living room. But the cops came to my office yesterday and accused me of killing her!" Michael huffed, exasperated.

He shrugged his shoulders and emitted a half-chuckle, half-sigh. He'd somehow become the poster boy for karma.

At Michael's arraignment later that day, Andrew pleaded "not guilty" on his client and best friend's behalf. Predictably, the prosecutor requested that Michael be tried for first-degree murder and held without bail until his trial date. Andrew vehemently argued against the proposition, citing Michael's spotless record and good standing in the community.

Nevertheless, the judge ruled and denied bail. With indisputable evidence and premeditated first-degree murder charge filed against him, Michael was going nowhere.

Michael nearly collapsed in shock. Andrew's eyes bulged out of their sockets. He knew there was precedence for such a decision but had never considered that it'd apply to Michael. All Andrew could do was place his arm on his buddy's shoulder. No words could provide any comfort in such a trying time. Despite all of his wealth and power, Michael couldn't punch his way out of a paper bag to freedom.

Although Michael avowed his innocence, he was arraigned by a judge and confined to Auburn Correctional Facility, a maximum-security prison in upstate New York. Michael would be incarcerated until his trial.

Chapter 27

7he following day, Michael was transported up to Auburn and led into in a containment area specially designed for new inmates. The guards removed his handcuffs and leg shackles and told him to strip naked for an examination by the attending physician.

His clothes were discarded and replaced with a charcoal gray prison uniform. He was permitted to keep only his watch and the Star of David hanging from his neck. Michael was assigned prison number 58123, then instructed to sign a document acknowledging his arrival date.

An armed guard reapplied the shackles to Michael's wrists and escorted him into another section of the prison, accessible only by lock and key. There were three floors of cells overlooking a courtyard in the center, and iron steps were positioned at each corner of the building.

As Michael slowly marched to his new home, shouts, whistles and the clanging of prison bars rang out. The prisoners celebrated the arrival of a new piece of flesh to their domain. Michael kept his head down, ignoring the calls, as he walked to his cell. When they finally reached his eight-by-ten foot cellblock on the second level, the guard removed a key from a chain at his side, unlocked the cell door, and removed the handcuffs from Michael's wrists.

Michael gazed at the spare amenities in his cell. It was a far cry from what he was accustomed to, to say the least. His sprawling, ten thousand square foot mansion had been replaced by a eight-by-ten cell that included only a bed, toilet, and sink—the barest of essentials.

The guards locked the door behind them and left Michael to adapt to his new surroundings.

As he sat on the bed, a voice from a neighboring cell called out, "What's your name pretty boy?"

Since Michael didn't respond, the inmate repeated, "I said—what's your name?"

"Michael," he responded in a soft-spoken voice.

"Speak up! I can't hear you!" demanded the inmate next door.

"I said, Michael."

"Michael who?"

"Michael Aronstein."

"Whatcha in for?"

"Murder, but I didn't do it."

"Yeah that's what they all say," he chuckled. "Where you from?"

"New York."

"New York is a big state. Whereabouts?" the prisoner asked.

"Kings Point."

"Isn't that by the water?"

"Yeah, I guess," Michael replied disgustedly.

Silence prevailed. Michael lied down on the bed, and a stream of thoughts ran through his mind. It wasn't supposed to be this way. Everything he'd worked so hard to achieve was going up in smoke. Where was his head? Maybe this can still work out in the end.

He closed his eyes and slowly drifted into a deep sleep, in which he dreamt of his family, huddled together, laughing their heads off.

A loud buzzing sound woke him from his slumber, as it was time for the prisoners to take their daily exercise out in the courtyard. One by one, the cell doors were opened, and armed guards escorted the prisoners outside in a single-file line.

The courtyard was fortified by a high barbed-wire fence. Armed guards sat atop a lookout tower, overlooking the grounds and scrutinizing the activities below. Picnic tables and basketball courts were scattered within its parameters.

Not knowing a soul, Michael sat down at the first open table he saw. While he assessed his new surroundings, another inmate joined him.

"Got a smoke?" asked the inmate.

"I don't smoke."

"I'm Jose. Who are you?"

"Michael."

"Haven't seen you around. You new?"

"Yeah."

"What brings you here?" Jose inquired.

"They say I committed murder, but I didn't do it. How about you?"

"Armed robbery," Jose said, with a hint of braggadocio. "I needed some cash to support my drug habit, so I knocked off a corner grocery store in my neighborhood and got caught."

"Where did you live?" Michael asked.

"Up in Harlem, near 168th street. Where you from?" he countered.

"Nassau County, over by the north shore in Long Island."

"Shit man, that's money country. What the fuck are you doin' in here? Don't you have enough scratch for a lawyer to keep you out of this joint?"

"I wish it was that easy," Michael replied, trailing off.

Another prisoner approached the bench and sat down. A cigarette wedged behind one ear, he cocked his head towards Michael and said, "I'm Pete, your neighbor from earlier."

When he extended his hand for a shake, Michael apprehensively reciprocated. Pete didn't look like a criminal. He had a lightly freckled face and reddish-grey crew cut.

"If you ever need some flour or sugar, just knock on my door," Pete joked. In his next breath, he asked, "How long they keepin' you?"

"I'm waiting for a trial date."

"Hell, they must have a lot of evidence stacked up against your ass if they put you in this shithole."

"What are you in for?" asked Michael.

"I'm doin' time for multiple burglaries. I was out of a job and needed cash to support my family. I tried to sell some stereos to an undercover cop, and he grabbed me."

Pete pulled the cigarette from his ear and lit the end. "Let's take a walk," he suggested. Michael accepted the proposal, but Jose declined and stayed behind.

"Wanna smoke?" Pete offered, as he pulled out a pack of Camel cigarettes and tapped it against the palm of his hand. Michael spotted a faded tattoo of a mermaid with the name "Cathy" inscribed on his right forearm.

"No thanks," Michael said.

"You ever been locked up before?" asked Pete.

"No, this is a first for me."

"Son, this is a whole new world your livin' in," he explained. "You gotta watch your ass wherever you go around here or these fucks will play you like a toy. They think they own the joint. Be very careful about what you say, how you say it, and who you're saying it to."

"Well how am I supposed to know who's who?"

"There are the bosses—you'll know 'em when you see 'em—and they all got their own followers and snitches. Those guys will rat your ass out at the drop of a hat and beat the livin' shit out of you unless they decide to recruit you. Watch out, cuz if you decline, they might take it as an insult," he warned.

"You think that's a good idea—to join them?" Michael asked, scared out of his wits.

"You look like a nice guy," Pete commented. "I'll keep an eye on you. Anybody bothers you, just let me know."

"Thanks," Michael replied.

The guards blew their whistles, notifying the inmates to return to their cells. As the guards escorted them back inside, Michael noticed some of the prisoners looking him up and down; he feared that his good looks had caught their attention.

Shrugging it off, Michael arrived at his cell, where a clean towel and a set of toiletries sat on his bed.

"Guard!" he shouted. Since no one responded, he yelled at the top of his lungs again. A guard finally appeared and stuck his face through the bars.

"What's the problem?"

"Can I get a magazine or newspaper to read?" The guard laughed under his breath.

"Do you think you're in some sort of hotel? There's no room service here, buddy. You're gonna have to wait until library period," he snickered.

With nothing else to do but drown in his sorrows, Michael lied back down on his bed and attempted to sleep his misery away. Dinnertime approached rather quickly. He was escorted with the other inmates to the mess hall.

Michael took his tray and stood in line. After receiving his cafeteria-style food, he looked around for a table with familiar faces. He spotted Pete and sat down in the seat across from him.

"How's your first day going, Mike?"

"I don't know if I can make it through another one," he complained.

"You'll get used to it," Pete assured him.

As Michael took a bite of his food, another, much bigger, inmate stopped at the table. "Why don't you introduce me to your new friend, Petey?"

"Yeah, Mike say hello to Vito," Pete said. "Vito, say hello to Mike." Michael stuck out his hand, but Vito just winked back at him.

"Who's that?" Michael asked after the baldheaded bull walked away. "Remember I told you about some of the bosses in this joint?"

"Yeah," Michael recalled.

"Well he's one of them. Try to avoid Vito if you can. He's no fuckin' good."

"Okay, thanks for the tip," Michael responded.

After dinner, they walked over to a cart and emptied their dishes, eating utensils, and trays. Michael looked over his shoulder and spied Vito standing right behind him. He acknowledged Michael with another wink and said, "See you later."

The next day, Michael was approached by one of Vito's lieutenants out in the courtyard. "Vito would like to see you."

Michael's heart began to throb, and a lump grew in his throat. He knew that he had no choice but to yield to his command. Michael reluctantly went over to where the boss held court.

"Hey, pretty boy," Vito greeted him. "How much time you doin'?"

"I really couldn't tell you. I'm still awaiting my day in court."

"For however many days you do have left in this shithole, you'll do just fine as long as you stay close to me and my boys," Vito assured him. "If not, life could get a little difficult, if you know what I mean." Michael nodded then walked off.

Several days passed before he encountered the brute again. An inmate approached Michael and relayed the message that Vito demanded to see him. Michael decided to stand up to him, rebuffing the request with little concern.

That evening, Michael went to the communal shower. He undressed and adjusted the spigot to his desired temperature. He was lathering his body with soap and shampoo, when one of the inmates shouted out, "Hey Jew Boy!"

Before Michael could respond to the call, he was savagely attacked. One inmate covered his mouth from behind, and another lifted his legs. They moved him to a secluded corner of the bathroom and took turns sodomizing him. Traumatized, Michael fainted.

The perpetrators quickly exited the scene and blended in with the rest of the prisoners. Fearing retaliation, Michael didn't report the incident. He told only his neighbor and trustworthy friend, Pete.

Chapter 28

While Michael struggled behind bars, Andrew worked tirelessly to prepare a defense for his dear friend. He hired Wally Summers, his trusted private investigator, to get to the bottom of the situation. Michael didn't care about the cost. He would have gone to any length to rid himself of these false accusations.

If anybody could uncover the real truth, it was Wally, a retired police detective who had tremendous experience with homicide cases. Andrew had used Wally many times for past cases and was consistently impressed by his ability to suss out the details that the cops missed.

Wally pored over Maria's background with a fine-toothed comb. He learned that she and her poor Mexican family immigrated to Harlem when she was very young. She managed to support herself despite dropping out of high school, chiefly by landing the waitressing job at the bar where she met Michael.

During his interview with her mother, Andrew discovered that Maria's brother had a criminal record. In fact, he had ties to a gang in Harlem, which led Andrew to believe that her murder could have been some sort of retaliation.

Maria herself didn't have a record, though she had dabbled with drugs here and there with some old friends. She kept close ties with her family and even gave them money every so often, supplementing the food stamps they received from the government.

Maria's boss at the cocktail lounge described her as a hard working and conscientious employee who hardly ever missed a shift. Wally also questioned her coworker, Angelina Esposito, who had a spotty background. Angelina was rumored to have worked as a prostitute in the past, but had only been arrested on misdemeanor drug charges. Since then, she'd been working on getting her life back together. Angelina told Wally that Maria occasionally saw some men other than Michael.

Wally followed that thread, questioning the security guard at her apartment building about her other visitors. The guard agreed to help, but could only release the sign-in records if there was a court-ordered subpoena.

Andrew petitioned the court to obtain the document, and intensely studied it with Wally, searching for some type of pattern. Michael's name was the most prevalent, but a man named Jose Gomez had also visited Maria on multiple occasions.

Now they had another person of interest, even though Gomez had stopped visiting about four months before Maria was killed. They were dumbfounded. The only person who entered her apartment on the day of her murder was Michael. They examined all of the visitors to the building on the day of her death, but their stories checked out.

Wally went on to check the employees' punch cards from that evening and even inquired about any outside contractors or utility workers who might have been in the building. The super had a master key, but his alibi held up as well.

Andrew acquired a subpoena for Maria's phone records, and he and Wally combed through every page in their search for the true perpetrator. But their efforts were fruitless.

They were up against a stone wall, and all of the evidence still pointed to Michael as the killer. Andrew visited the prison with hopes of persuading Michael to own up to the crime and cop a plea deal to save his life. But Michael insisted that he was innocent. He believed, perhaps fool heartedly, that the justice system would ultimately prevail in his favor after the facts were laid out at the trial.

Chapter 29

*M*onths slowly passed, and Michael had no choice but to acclimate to prison life and its daily routines as best as he could. After he obtained library privileges, life became somewhat more tolerable. He was assigned mess hall and laundry duties, just like any other inmate in the facility. There was no class distinction within the prison walls.

Despite his dire circumstances, Michael remained optimistic. He held onto the hope that he'd be found innocent at trial and released, though his hearing was still weeks away. Andrew was one of the best criminal lawyers that money could buy. Why buck the system? Just suck it up and don't create any problems, he thought to himself.

The letters from his parents, Becky, and, most of all, his children, provided respite from his grueling existence. Though Michael occasionally became even more despondent as he read their missives.

After three months behind bars, Michael was granted the privilege of receiving visitors other than his lawyer, the first of whom were his parents.

Visibly distraught, Sadie picked up the telephone on her side of the thick glass partition. Her son's predicament had severely weathered her appearance. Herbie sat next to her, attempting to remain stoic.

"Michael, my son. How are you?" asked his mother.

"I'm doing the best I can, considering the circumstances."

"Are they treating you okay?" she inquired.

"If I tried to complain, nobody would listen to me anyway."

"You look terrible—so thin and so pale," she observed. "Are they feeding you alright? You look tired. Are you getting enough sleep?"

Michael stared back in silence. He couldn't bear to answer such questions. Tears began to stream from his mother's eyes, while Herbie maintained a grave expression.

"The children have been asking about you. They miss you terribly. They want to know when you'll be coming home," Sadie uttered.

She passed the phone to her husband and retreated to the corner, crying hysterically.

His father sobbed, "Why did you do it, Michael? You have everything in the world to live for!" he exclaimed. "Such a beautiful wife and children. A bright future still lies ahead of you. How could you do this to your family?"

Michael couldn't hold his composure. He pushed out his chair and stood up to leave without any parting words. Only tears.

He reentered his cell and collapsed into his cot, drying his face on his pillow. Images of his children flew through his mind: Abbey riding her tricycle down the driveway in Kings Point, the children all dressed up on Halloween with pillow cases at the ready, gently guiding his Julia's tiny hand through a serve on their tennis court.

Everything hit him all at once. On top of being separated from his family, he'd lose his fortune. The mansion, his cars, everything. What he worked so hard to achieve.

Suddenly, the emotions building up inside of him erupted like a volcano. With one swift swipe of his arm, he knocked all of his personal effects from a small table onto the floor and proceeded to vigorously stomp them to pieces. He shook the cell bars in a violent rage, as if he was trying to pry them loose.

"Get me the hell out of here!" he shouted to nobody in particular. "I DIDN'T DO IT, GODDAMN IT!"

Chapter 30

D ue to the immense backlog in the court system, Michael's trial date was delayed until June of 1968. In municipal courtroom 205A in lower Manhattan, the prosecution and defense attorneys questioned and selected potential jurors. After eliminating those who opposed capital punishment or were unsuitable for various other reasons, the lawyers selected a jury panel.

Reporters, friends, family, and a slew of curious citizens packed the courtroom. Michael, dressed in a suit and tie, sat at the defense's table beside Andrew. To their right sat the prosecutor, Joseph Cortez, and his assistant, Nancy McCormack. Cortez was a bright, young attorney, eager to make a name for himself by winning a high-profile case like Michael's.

Michael turned around and scanned the courtroom. He spotted his parents and sister but didn't see his wife or children. The chatter throughout the room increased as more attendees entered.

Finally, the bailiff announced, "Please rise for the honorable Judge Stephen Prince." Silence fell over the room as the judge emerged from his chambers. He summoned both the defense and prosecuting attorneys to the bench.

They spoke briefly for a couple of minutes, and the lawyers returned to their respective desks. The judge pounded the gavel and called the court to order, announcing: "The People of New York versus Michael Aronstein."

Judge Prince first called on the prosecution to present its opening arguments. Mr. Cortez paced back and forth across the room as he addressed the jury.

"Ladies and gentleman of the jury, the state intends to prove beyond a shadow of doubt that Mr. Michael Aronstein planned and executed the murder of Ms. Maria Salvatez. We will present indisputable facts to support our case, and, piece-by-piece, you will learn how and why he ended, not only this innocent woman's life, but also her unborn child's. Faced with the prospect of losing his family as a result of this bastard's birth, Michael Aronstein opted to take matters into his own hands. I am confident that you will find the defendant guilty of all charges. Thank you."

"Your floor, Mr. Fox," the judge directed.

Andrew stood up and walked towards the jury stand. Cloaked in a dapper custom-tailored suit, he looked and dressed the part of a high-powered criminal attorney. If nothing else, that was sure to impress a few jurors.

"Ladies and gentleman, my name is Andrew Fox, and I represent Mr. Michael Aronstein. Contrary to what Mr. Cortez has told you, the supposed facts of this case are far from indisputable. I will present evidence that proves that Mr. Aronstein did NOT commit this crime. Furthermore, you will hear extensive testimonies to Michael's true character, after which you will clearly see that the wrong man is on trial. Thank you for your time."

"Mr. Cortez, please call your first witness." the judge directed.

"The people would like to call Mr. Lucian Smith to the stand." A middle-aged man of dark complexion arose and walked towards the bench. The bailiff presented a bible and swore him in.

"Can you please state your name for the court?" asked Cortez.

"My name is Lucian Smith."

"Mr. Smith, what do you do for a living?"

"I'm a security guard and doorman at the Madison Terrace Apartments."

"Where is that located?"

"The corner of 49th and Madison."

"For how long have you worked there?"

"Past twenty years, sir."

"Are you familiar with all of the tenants in the building?"

"Just said I been there twenty years. I better know 'em all."

"Okay, let me rephrase that. Did you know a tenant named Maria Salvatez?"

"I certainly did," said Lucian.

"Were you on duty the night of April 22, 1967?" the prosecutor continued.

"Yes," he replied. "It was pouring outside, so I helped Maria carry some groceries up to her apartment that evening. She gave me a stuffed animal to give to my little girl."

"When you dropped off the groceries, was anybody else in the apartment?"

"Not to my knowledge," replied Lucian.

"I have here a log of the date, time, and signature of every visitor who entered the day of the killing. Do you recognize it?" the prosecutor asked.

"I do," he replied.

"I present Exhibit A," Cortez announced. "Mr. Smith, please confirm that there are names printed next to each signature."

"Yes sir," he replied.

"Please read the names aloud to the court." Lucian started reading the names. When he got to the bottom of the page, he uttered, "Michael Aronstein."

There was a hush in the courtroom.

Mr. Cortez continued, "Do you know this man?" Lucian pointed at Michael. "Did you see him enter Madison Terrace Apartments that evening?"

"Yes, I did. That's Mr. Aronstein, alright."

A burst of chatter filled the room. The judge pounded his gavel, calling for order in the courtroom.

Lucian continued, "Michael used to come by quite often. Though on that particular night, he didn't stay very long. I remember him leaving after only 20 minutes."

"And how did he look as he exited the building?"

"Agitated. Distraught, I guess."

"Was he in a hurry?"

"Not particularly. Mr. Aronstein was usually in-and-out. No fuss."

That wasn't quite the damning portrait that Cortez was looking for. Lucian had thrown in some other details that must have seemed extraneous to him when they had prepared his testimony beforehand.

"Your witness," Cortez said.

Andrew approached the witness stand for the cross-examination.

"Mr. Smith," he asked, "how long did you know Maria Salvatez?"

"Approximately two years," he stated.

"What shift do you usually work?"

"I come in at 6:00 PM and stay through the night into the early morning," he explained.

"Did Ms. Salvatez ever host any other guests besides Mr. Aronstein in those two years?"

"Yes, she did. Quite alot."

"Did any of these individuals visit her multiple times, in the wee hours of the morning?"

"Now what does that matter?" asked Smith.

"I mean, do you think that Ms. Salvatez could had any other boyfriends?"

"Objection, your honor," the prosecution yelled out. "This is totally irrelevant. We all have the right to engage in romantic relationships."

"Overruled," ordered the judge. Please continue, Mr. Fox."

"Mr. Smith, do you believe that Ms. Salvatez had another boyfriend in addition to Michael Aronstein?"

"Yes, there was one other man," he answered.

"Can you elaborate a little further?"

"She would often leave a key at the front desk for another fella," he stated.

"Have you seen him lately? "

"No, it's been a while," he answered.

"Could he have entered Madison Terrace without your knowledge on that evening, April 22nd?"

"It's possible, but not very likely. Unless Maria rode the elevator down to the lobby and let him in while I was on my bathroom break."

"No further questions," Andrew said. He returned to his seat.

"Mr. Cortez, please call your next witness," the judge requested.

"The people would like to call Dorothea Augustus to the stand." Dorothea, an elderly, Greek-American woman with thick glasses, approached the witness stand.

"Please state your name for the court."

"My name is Dorothea Augustus."

"Ms. Augustus, where do you reside?"

"I live at Madison Terrace Apartments," she answered.

"And what is your apartment number?"

"That'd be 1-1-0-2." Dorothea clearly enunciated each digit.

"What is the proximity of your unit to that of the late Ms. Salvatez?"

"She was my next door neighbor."

"Can you tell us your account of the evening that Ms. Salvatez was killed?"

"I was in my apartment watching television when I heard an argument going on next door. After a little while, the front door of Maria's apartment slammed shut, and Mr. Aronstein left."

"How did you know it was Mr. Aronstein?"

"I saw him storming down the hallway, through the peephole of my front door."

"Well, what happened next?"

"A couple of minutes passed, and there was another knock at her door. It sounded as though she opened her door and let him back in. It was quiet, until I heard another commotion. The door slammed shut again, and I saw that Mr. Aronstein leaving through the peephole one more time." She paused. "You know you have to pass my apartment in order to catch the elevator," she added.

"At what time did this second visit occur?"

"It was around 10 o'clock," she replied with absolute certainty.

"Can you remember what Mr. Aronstein was wearing that night?"

"Absolutely. He wore a tan trench coat," she said.

Mr. Cortez instructed his associate to display the coat to the court.

"Is this the coat that Mr. Aronstein was wearing that night?" the prosecutor asked.

"Yes," she answered.

"Let it serve as Exhibit B," the prosecutor said. "No further questions."

"Your witness, Mr. Fox," said the judge. Andrew approached the stand.

"Ms. Augustus, what was the weather like that evening you saw Mr. Aronstein in your apartment building?"

"It was a rainy night. Downright miserable."

"Would you say that a lot of men in your building wore trench coats that evening?"

"Oh yes! It was pouring outside. I remember Mr. Weber in apartment 1112 had one just like it."

"So how can you be absolutely sure that it wasn't someone else in that tan trench coat that evening?"

"Because I saw the side of his face, and it was definitely Mr. Aronstein." The crowd rumbled.

"Were you wearing your glasses that evening?"

"No, I was not."

"Then how can you stand before this court and attest to the fact that you saw Mr. Aronstein leave the apartment if your sight was impaired?"

"I had my contacts in that evening." The spectators tried to stifle their chuckles.

"No further questions," Andrew uttered in frustration.

The court proceedings adjourned for the day and Andrew had to try to bolster a new defense strategy for his client.

Chapter 31

7he financial state of Michael's household crumbled as a result of his incarceration. Of course, he was terminated from Jones Bailey.

Michael had always taken care of the money on his own, leaving Lauren completely in the dark. She was shocked to find, on her first examination of their financial records, that there was an enormous amount of money tied up in assets—the mansion, summer home, cars, a boat—but relatively little in savings accounts. His real estate was mortgaged to the hilt. Michael had been living his version of the "high life," spending a disproportional amount of his money while convincing himself that the well would never run dry.

With the loss of Michael's income and the additional expense of his legal fees, Lauren resigned to drastically alter the family's lifestyle.

She put the summer home in the Hamptons on the block. The luxurious cars, which included a Mercedes convertible sports car and a Chrysler Imperial, were sold and replaced by a used station wagon. The country club membership, which they so dearly cherished, was cancelled. Private schools were switched to public schools. Lauren had to relieve Mia of her duties, as well; a fixture of the household disappeared. Embarrassed, shunned, and financially strapped, Lauren finally had no choice but to sell the sprawling mansion.

The night before the moving van was to arrive, Lauren, Mia, and the children packed up all of their belongings. They came across some boxes of photo albums in the attic. They gathered together in the family room, which was now sparsely furnished with sealed boxes, and reminisced as they looked over the old pictures.

"Look, Mom!" yelled Julia, as she pointed to some black-and-whites from Halloween. "You look just like the lion in the Wizard of Oz," she added. "Look at Dad. He looks so silly as the Scarecrow!" Everybody laughed. They continued shuffling through the pages of the album.

"Wow! Look how old I got since that picture in Jamaica! And how much the kids have grown," remarked Mia.

"Who's that, Mom?" asked Abbey.

"That's a picture of your father and me on our honeymoon," replied Lauren, as tears began to stream from her eyes. The children clutched their arms around her to give support.

"It'll be alright," Abbey whispered, as she wiped her mother's tears away with a tissue.

"Hey Mom, look at this one," said Brittney, doing her best to cheer up her mother. It was a picture of their old dog Buffy, a tan cocker spaniel.

"How cute," Lauren said. "I remember Daddy used to take her for daily walks, but she still managed to make in the house anyway."

"It would drive him crazy." They all collapsed in laughter.

"Can I take just one picture with me before you close it up?" asked Mia.

"You can take whatever you want," Lauren offered.

Now virtually a single mother of three, Lauren swallowed her pride and made some compromises. She sought a job as an elementary schoolteacher in order to support the family. Having her parents, as well as Sadie and Herbie, nearby helped her cope with the enormous workload. Both sets of grandparents pitched in to assist whenever they could. They even offered to watch the children for the evening if Lauren wanted to go out.

Lauren took them up on their offer one night in late October. She met her friend Toby for dinner at their favorite deli back in the old neighborhood on Long Island. They sat in their favorite booth and enjoyed the familiar sights nearly as much as the meal.

"Lauren, honey, how are things?" Toby's voice took on a softer tone. Though they had been catching up for the past twenty minutes, Toby sensed it was time to move beyond the casual small talk. During the tough times, Toby had remained a trusted friend and confidant of Lauren's, but still found it difficult to get her to open up.

"I'm doing—okay."

"Sure doesn't seem like it. This isn't the Lauren I remember. Have you been out of the house much? You used to love to buzz all around town." Lauren genuinely smiled for the first time all day.

"I did, didn't I?" She took a bite of her sandwich. "I do need to get some of my old energy back. I'll admit it."

"You have to accept that Michael is gone—possibly forever. I know it's tough to hear, but it's time for you to start moving on. Maybe go on a few dates?"

"Oh, God. That's the last thing on my mind right now."

"Well maybe it shouldn't be." Lauren took her friends words to heart. It was true; she hadn't ever thought about finding another companion. Michael had been her first and only boyfriend.

167

Later that night, Lauren examined herself in the mirror, sizing herself up as if she were a potential suitor. As was often the case, her thoughts drifted to Michael.

The early days of his courtship. The long talks they had in the late night hours, whispering over the phone, careful not to wake up their families. The dates to the bowling alley, drive-in movies, and the diner. Cheering on Andrew as he quarterbacked the football team to the playoffs. Spending long weekends in each other's company. Watching Michael pitch shutouts with bated breath.

Lauren stepped away from the mirror and pulled open a drawer on Michael's side of the bureau. She dug through a few pairs of dress socks and removed her wedding ring. She put it on, shut her eyes, and collapsed onto Michael's side of the bed.

Back in high school, Lauren had worn Michael's high school ring around her neck as proof that they were going steady. They were glued at the hip. One couldn't move without the other. Whether it was walking down the corridor together between classes or simply holding hands on the stroll to the bus stop after school let out. It was their routine. It was much simpler when Michael didn't even have time to see other girls.

On sunny weekend afternoons, they'd nestle together on a blanket by the river's edge, watching the crew practice for their school's team. They took full advantage of the privacy, caressing every inch of each other's bodies and locking lips with reckless abandon. They would talk about their schoolwork, gossip about friends, and sketch out their future together.

Although Lauren was fully devoted to Michael back in those days, she still resisted completely giving herself up, physically, hoping to save that special moment for their honeymoon. He could get frisky out there on the riverbed, but Lauren firmly deterred his advances each time.

Lauren smiled, bounced up from the bed, and stepped back in front of the mirror. She looked pretty good for her age, she thought. Who would walk away from this? Sometimes she blamed herself for pushing Michael away, but on a deeper level she knew that the real problem was with him.

His relentless sex drive had seemed ordinary at the time. It was commonplace for a teenage guy to press his girlfriend into doing the deed. That's just how they were programmed. Michael tried everything, even going so far as to whisper "I love you" into her ear—for the first time—as they cuddled on the sofa one Saturday night when her parents were out. When sweetness didn't work, he'd get angry.

A few months into their relationship, Michael and Lauren spent a Thursday afternoon in the library. They sat on opposite sides of a large table, Lauren leaning back in her chair as she leafed through a copy of *Hamlet*, and Michael hunched forward, struggling to keep his eyes off of her. He stroked her calf with his under the table, eliciting a smile and a playful return kick from Lauren.

"Stop it, Michael," she said with mock anger.

"Stop what?" he shot back.

"You know."

"Looks like you could use a break. Let's take a walk," he said with a sly cock of his head.

"But it's cold out."

"You can wear my jacket on top of yours, if you want."

He stood up and draped his coat over Lauren's shoulder, beckoning her to come along. Unable to resist, Lauren arose and hooked onto his arm. They stepped into the stairwell, where

Michael led her down the stairs to the dingy basement. He took his coat off of her shoulder and spread it out on the cold concrete floor. Lauren could sense what he was getting at, but nevertheless followed his lead.

As expected, the situation escalated. Kissing Michael and feeling the firm clutch of his hands on her backside made Lauren melt inside. She relented to his advances, let him unbutton anything he wanted. But as Lauren's dress slid off her shoulders, a cold chill came over her and snapped her out of the blissful trance.

"Wait, Michael. We can't. Not now."

Without a word, he pulled back and shot her a glare. His big blue eyes gave off a mix of anger and disappointment, boring a hole into her heart.

At the time, Lauren was upset and mildly alarmed, but she had brushed it off as an uncharacteristic outburst. Maybe that had been the first warning sign.

Chapter 32

The court reconvened on the following day.

"Please call your next witness, Mr. Cortez," Judge Prince ordered.

"The people would like to call Angelina Esposito." Dressed in spiked high heels, Angelina strolled up to the stand. She recited the oath and repeated her name while chomping on a wad of gum.

"Please describe your relationship with Maria Salvatez."

"I was one of Maria's closet friends."

"How long did you know the deceased?"

"About five years," she replied, as tears welled up in her eyes.

"How did the two of you meet?" asked Mr. Cortez.

Wiping the tears with a tissue, she answered, "At a cocktail lounge on the Lower Eastside. We both worked as waitresses."

"As close friends were you able to confide in one another?"

"What do you mean by that?"

"I mean, did you ever tell each other secrets that you didn't want anybody else to know?"

"Of course."

"Can you tell us any secrets that may pertain to this case?"

She began, "I knew that Maria was seeing this guy for a while. I gathered that he did something in finance, but she never told me where he worked. It seemed like he did very well for himself. He consistently surprised her with gifts, took her out to fancy restaurants, and even paid for her place at the Madison Terrace Apartments."

"How long did this relationship last?" Mr. Cortez asked.

"To my knowledge, about three years,"

"During their relationship, did Maria ever complain about Mr. Aronstein?"

"Just before her murder, she told me that she was a few months pregnant with his baby. And she wanted to keep it."

The courtroom buzzed with excitement. Judge Prince pounded his gavel to restore order. "Okay, let's continue," the judge demanded.

"No further questions," said Cortez.

As shocked by this revelation as anyone, Andrew whispered in Michael's ear. "Why didn't you tell me about this?"

"It wasn't mine," he shot back.

Visibly shaken, Andrew stepped up to cross-examine the witness.

"Ms. Esposito, have you ever been arrested?"

"Yes"

"Objection, your honor," shouted the prosecutor. "This has no relevance to the case," he complained.

"Objection sustained. Please have it stricken from the record," he instructed.

"Okay, next question. Where do you live, Ms. Esposito?"

"At 65th and Park."

"How can you afford to live in such a high rent district on a waitress's salary?"

"Ex-cuuuse me?" Angelina hissed.

"I asked how you finance your posh lifestyle, Ms. Esposito. How you can afford expensive low-cut tops and miniskirts like the ones you're wearing at this very moment."

"I don't appreciate what you're implyin'."

The crowd rumbled at the early signs of drama.

"Objection, your honor. This questioning is irrelevant," Mr. Cortez declared.

"Sustained. Counselor, keep your questioning within the parameters of this case," the judge directed. Andrew nodded and returned his attention to Angelina.

"Ms. Esposito, did Maria have relationships with any other men during this three year affair with the defendant?"

"I can't say for sure. Waitresses get hit on all the time. I couldn't follow Maria into her bedroom every night, if you know what I mean."

"Fair enough. No further questions," Andrew said, annoyed.

"Would the prosecution like to call any other witnesses?" asked Judge Prince.

"Yes your honor," replied Mr. Cortez. "The people would like to call Detective Timothy Fitzgerald."

The gruff, redheaded detective lumbered up to the stand.

"Detective Fitzgerald, what is your background in law enforcement?"

"I've worked for the New York City Police Department for over twenty years, and now I head up the homicide division. I was in charge of this case."

"What happened on the evening of April 22nd, 1967?"

"We were summoned to the apartment of the deceased, Maria Salvatez, at the Madison Terrace Apartments to investigate a probable homicide. We found her sprawled out on her bedroom floor, naked, with several large bruises on her body."

"What was the official the cause of death?"

"Strangulation, sir. No doubt about it."

"In what condition was her apartment?"

"It was pretty well intact, except for the bedroom, which showed signs of a struggle. There were also some drawers left open."

"Were any items missing from the crime scene?"

"We were unable to determine if a robbery had occurred. It seemed like someone had rummaged through her underwear drawer, since it had been left open. A stray pair was also sitting on the floor."

"Did you find any fingerprints?"

"Yes, the defendant's prints were all over the apartment. We found a button that matched his trench coat and an umbrella with the initials *M.A.* inscribed on the handle."

"Had there been any tampering with the front door?"

"There were no signs of forcible entry. It's likely that the victim knew the perpetrator and willingly let him—or her, I guess—into the apartment."

"Are there any other exits in the apartment through which an attacker could have escaped?"

"No, sir."

"Thank you, Mr. Fitzgerald. I have nothing else, your honor," Mr. Cortez said.

"Would the defense like to cross examine this witness?" Judge Prince inquired.

"Yes, I would, your honor," responded Andrew. He casually walked up to the stand with his right hand in his pants pocket.

"Mr. Fitzgerald, during your investigation, did you find any other fingerprints that did not match Mr. Aronstein's?"

"Yes, we did."

"And whose were they?"

"We searched our records but couldn't find a match."

"How about the coat button? Are you absolutely sure that it belonged to the defendant?"

"Well, it matched all of the others."

"Were there any buttons missing from my client's coat when he was arrested?"

"No, but he could have easily replaced it with one of the spares sewn into the inside of the coat."

"Did you find any spare buttons in his coat?"

"I-I'm not sure if we checked," the detective stammered.

"Thank you Mr. Fitzgerald. I have nothing else at this time."

The prosecution called Freddie Burrows to the stand. There he was, bald, fat Freddie. Michael was astonished to see his old pal waddle up to the stand..

"Mr. Burrows, what is your relationship to the defendant?"

"I've known Michael since way, way back—in Brooklyn. We palled around and partied together."

"Where do you reside nowadays?" Cortez continued.

"In Nevada."

"And what brings you to this court today?"

"A few months ago, I read about Michael's case in the newspaper. I was totally shocked once I realized that it was the same Michael Aronstein from back in Brooklyn.. But then I recalled running into him and Maria in Las Vegas some time ago during a real estate convention."

"What was so peculiar about that?" Mr. Cortez inquired.

"Objection," Andrew called out. "Leading the witness."

"Sustained," Judge Prince said.

Cortez rephrased his question, "What were the circumstances of that encounter?"

"When I bumped into them in the hotel elevator, Michael acted kind of strange and evasive. But what stunned me the most was the shiner under Maria's eye. She had tried to conceal it behind sunglasses, but at some point they fell off. It looked as though someone punched her right in the eye. She was pretty quiet and appeared fearful of mentioning the bruise."

"Did you notice anything else peculiar in Mr. Aronstein's behavior that night?"

"Yes, later on I saw Michael at the blackjack table, drunk as a skunk, with chips stacked up to the ceiling and what looked like two hookers by his side. He was beaming from head to toe."

Freddie reached into his jacked pocket and pulled out a picture.

"Here, I even brought this photo along. I took it when he wasn't looking because I couldn't believe my own eyes."

The spectators roared in disbelief, and Andrew had a look of disgust written all over his face.

The prosecution's final witness, Dr. Eugene Costello of the coroner's office, was called to the stand. He testified that the autopsy revealed the cause of death as suffocation, and that a fetus was discovered in Maria's womb.

After that bombshell, the prosecution rested. Judge Prince called the court to order and asked Andrew to call his first witness.

"I would like to call Mr. Sirhan Obatta to the stand."

Mr. Obatta, a turban fixed atop his head, proceeded to the stand to be sworn in. After Sirhan recited the required oath and confirmed his name, Andrew launched into his line of questioning.

"Mr. Obatta, what is your occupation?"

"I am a taxi driver," he responded in his British Indonesian accent.

"And who is your employer?"

"Metro Cab Company."

"How long have you worked there?"

"About five years, give or take a couple of months."

"Were you working on the night of April 22, 1967?"

"Yes, I was on duty in midtown Manhattan."

"Did you pick up any passengers at Madison Terrace Apartments that evening?"

"Yes I did."

"Is there a record of the fares you received?"

"Yes, of course. Metro keeps detailed records." he proudly responded.

Andrew pulled a sheet of paper from the inside pocket of his sport jacket.

"I present Exhibit C," he said. "Mr. Obatta, please describe how these records are obtained."

"Well, after we pick up a fare, we call it into our dispatcher, and he records the trip."

"And at approximately what time did Mr. Aronstein enter your cab that evening?"

"It was 9:37 PM."

"Please let the record show that the fare log affirms this statement," Andrew said. "Mr. Obatta, please continue detailing the events as you remember them."

"It was a very stormy night. He asked me to take him to the downtown financial district, where his car was parked outside an office building. On the way, we stopped off at a drug store. When we arrived to his final destination, Mr. Aronstein handed me a hundred dollar bill, but I couldn't make change. And no banks were open at that hour. So he gave me a fifty-dollar tip. Biggest one I ever got," he chuckled.

"Did anything else of note happen during that cab ride?"

"No sir," he replied.

177

"No further questions," said Andrew. The judge asked the prosecutors if they wanted to cross-examine this witness. They passed.

"Your next witness, please, Mr. Fox."

"Yes your honor, I would like to recall Ms. Dorothea Augustus to the stand."

Dorothea Augustus made her way back up to the witness stand.

"Ms. Augustus, you testified earlier that you saw my client Mr. Aronstein leave at approximately 10:00 PM. Is that correct?" Andrew asked.

"Yes, sir."

"How can you be sure that was the exact time?"

"It's easy," she said. "My favorite show, The Red Skelton Hour, airs every Thursday at 10:00 PM. I never miss it."

"Then can you explain how you saw Mr. Aronstein outside your door at 10:00 PM if he was in a cab at 9:37PM?"

There was an outbreak in the courtroom. Judge Prince struck his gavel and summoned the court to order.

"No further questions," Andrew stated, as Mr. Cortez and his assistant huddled up at their table, strategizing their damage control.

"Mr. Cortez, would you like to cross-examine this witness?" the judge asked.

"No, your honor," replied the prosecutor.

"Mr. Fox, do you have any other witnesses you would like to call to the stand at this time?

"Yes your honor, I would like to call Mr. Thomas Phillips to the stand," A blue- collar worker wearing his Sunday best rose in his seat and made his way to the front of the courtroom.

"Mr. Phillips can you tell the court who is your employer?" Andrew began.

"The Universal Meter Company, sir."

"And for how long have you worked for Universal?"

"Fifteen long years," Phillips answered.

"What do you do for Universal?"

"I service and certify that the meters are accurate to protect the company from any fraudulent behavior by its drivers. The state requires every taxi service operating in the state of New York to receive a certification once a year in order to maintain its license.."

"Have you ever inspected meter # JQ5731289SL which is located in Cab 1876, the cab in which Mr. Aronstein was a passenger on the night of April 22,1967?"

"Yes indeed. I have"

"What was the certification number issued to that meter?"

"It was 85976113"

"And the date of inspection?"

"July 11ᵗʰ 1967"

"Did the inpection show any flaws or problems with the meter?"

"No, not that I am aware of. If it had, it wouldn't have passed inspection"

"Is it possible that the clock in the meter could have malfunctioned?"

"As I said, if I found any problems with the meter I would not have issued a certificate "

"I'm done with the witness your honor"

Frustrated, Andrew went back to his chair with a tail between his legs.

"Would you like to cross examine the witness Mr. Cortez?"

"No your honor"

Another witness, an employee of a drug store near Maria's apartment, was called to the stand and testified that Michael

179

purchased makeup from his store. The clerk unmistakably identified Michael as the customer, pointing a finger directly at his face.

In the weeks to come, many character witnesses testified before the court on Michael's behalf. Fellow coworkers and members of his synagogue described him as charitable, caring, and an all-around great guy.

To conclude the trial, each side presented its closing arguments. Mr. Cortez strolled towards the jury box. With his hands comfortably at his sides, he stared directly into the jurors' faces, commanding their undivided attention.

"Ladies and gentlemen of the jury, I have presented indisputable evidence that proves that Michael Aronstein is a cold and calculating killer. On that fateful night back in April of 1967, he murdered an innocent young woman who had everything to live for. His motive? Pure and simple—it was greed. He knew that if Maria were alive today, the truth about his infidelity and bastard child would have been exposed. He would have lost his fortune, family, and fame. His unblemished reputation would have been shattered. He had everything to lose. Not only did he kill his secret lover, he also took the life of an innocent unborn child, all to try to cover up his terrible mistake."

Mr. Cortez, a devout Catholic, thought that line might sway some of the more religious jury members.

"This is not a man who simply had an extramarital affair. His controlling nature, coupled with his abusive behavior towards Maria, led him to commit this heinous crime. He saw no other way out of it. He asked Maria to give up the baby, and when she refused, he knew darned well that everything he'd worked so hard for was about to go up in smoke. His mind was distorted by purely selfish motives. He was evil, manipulative, and deceitful.

When you deliberate, please think of the two souls who lost their lives because of the actions of this cold-blooded killer."

Cortez walked away, confident that he'd made one of the best closing arguments of his career. It was Andrew's turn to address the jury. He was dressed conservatively, in a three-piece Hickey Freeman suit with the gold chain of a pocket watch dangling from his vest's side pocket.

This was the most important case he'd ever tried. It was a do-or-die situation. His best friend's life was dangling in the air, and he had to put on an Oscar-worthy performance. He approached the jury stand with his head bowed in deep concentration. He took a moment to gather his thoughts and gain his composure, and then launched into his closing arguments.

"Ladies and gentlemen of the jury, contrary to some of the testimony you've heard over the course of this trial, Michael Aronstein is a model father and a community leader held in high esteem by his peers on Wall Street. He is not a cold-blooded killer. This is a man who has never committed a single crime, outside of getting a few parking tickets. He has never—in all his life—struck any human being with malice. His kindness, generosity, and wisdom have had a positive impact on countless individuals' lives.

There were just too many inconsistencies in the prosecution's case for you to convict him of this crime. The puzzle pieces don't connect—the evidence, circumstantial. The number of witnesses who put their reputations on the line to defend Mr. Aronstein is, in itself, is a testament to his superior character. The only crime my client is guilty of is infidelity, which certainly does not warrant a punishment of this magnitude. Ladies and gentlemen, if you have a single ounce of compassion for this individual, you will find him not guilty of these charges."

He walked back to the table and patted Michael on the back. All they could do was wait for the jurors' verdict.

Five weeks had passed since Michael's trial began. After several days of deliberation, the jury came to a unanimous decision. The court was packed with photographers and spectators waiting anxiously for the verdict.

"Do you have a verdict?" the judge asked the foreman of the jury.

"We do, Your Honor."

"Will the defendant please rise?"

The bailiff took a slip of paper from the foreman and gave it to the judge.

The foreman read, "We find the defendant Michael Aronstein guilty of murder in the first degree. He is to be sentenced to death, as deemed by the laws of the State of New York."

A hush of silence came over the courtroom after the announcement. Michael rested his head on the desk, outwardly sobbing, and Andrew leaned over to embrace him. Michael's parents and sister wept uncontrollably. Michael was shackled and escorted out of the courtroom, back to Auburn Correctional Facility to await his execution. His luck had finally run out.

Chapter 33

After the sentencing, the noose around Michael's neck tightened; he was reassigned to the isolated, high-security cellblock on death row that housed the electric chair. Dubbed "the fryer," it had cooked more convicts than any other in the state.

Life in prison became almost unbearable. He was confined to his cell for twenty-three hours per day instead of twelve. All of his hopes of vindication were snuffed away.

Isolated from the general prison population, Michael could only interact with the guards or the handful of convicts who shared the same fate. His outdoor exercise was limited to a strategically confined area. He and his new neighbors on Death Row were the only ones likely to make a near-impossible escape attempt. They had nothing left to lose.

Michael's new cell contained a bed, toilet, and sink. Meals were served directly to his quarters, and he was limited to just one visitation at certain designated intervals. He was stripped of all his work duties, and his library privileges were revoked. Rehabilitation was no longer an option.

As the years lapsed, Michael grew depressed and hardened. He was frail and haggard. His outgoing and happy-go-lucky personality disappeared, and he developed a twitch in his right thumb as a result of the emotional trauma. Thoughts of suicide entered his mind, but he couldn't fathom how to go about taking his own life. Plus, if he took that drastic step, that slim chance of the real killer surfacing would vanish.

The only thing that kept him from total insanity was reading. From time to time, he requested that material be sent to his cell. When he couldn't sleep, reading magazines and outdated newspapers provided him some solace. He read books on Judaism and made it a habit to recite the Shema to himself every night before going to bed. He wrote letters to friends and family to keep his mind occupied. Receiving the occasional response from his children or parents was too often the highlight of many months' time.

To break the monotony, he'd often listen to his favorite old tunes on a portable cassette player. He habitually played the song "You're A Star", the song to which he and his mother had danced at his Bar Mitzvah.

His memories of the affair were still crystal clear. He had flawlessly recited his Bar Mitzvah prayers, read from the Torah, and entered into manhood before a large audience of relatives and fellow congregants. The countless hours he had spent studying and practicing had paid off. He couldn't help but think of his present circumstances, in which tireless study was his only repose from the tortuously empty days behind bars.

Rabbi Sakowitz had lauded Michael's spectacular achievement before directing the guests into the decorated auditorium for a catered luncheon. Jubilation filled the air as the bandleader struck up the traditional Jewish Hora tune. Everybody danced in a revolving circle, stepping one foot over the other, all in celebration of Michael and his family. He could still feel the motion of his chair bobbing up and down as some of the bigger men lifted him to the sky. Clinging on for dear life,

Michael smiled wide, his face illuminated by the light reflected off the glass chandelier just a few inches from his head.

After the salad course, his mother requested a special slow dance. The band went into a song entitled, "You're a Star". Its lyrics held significant meaning; Sadie had hoped all of her guests would take note of how they applied to Michael. The bandleader belted out the first few notes, and Michael and his mother took center stage on the dance floor.

It began with the words:

It's your birthday today
You've grown up in every way
Through the laughter and the tears
You have blossomed through the years
You're so kind and so bright
And you're everyone's delight
You're a star
And we'll always love you-----------

There wasn't a dry eye in the room when they left the dance floor. Michael had never gotten so many hugs, kisses and attention from so many people in one day.

He felt like a celebrity in his new Bar Mitzvah suit, with the photographer's lights flashing in his eyes. Chanukah had arrived early that year; gifts and envelopes bulged out of the pockets of his suit jacket.

Only now, in his decrepit state, could he fully appreciate all that his parents, who came from little means, had done for him. He picked up the watch his parents had given him on that special day. Even after all of these years, both good and bad, Michael still kept it by his bed. The back of the watch was inscribed with the words "We Love You" and the date of his Bar Mitzvah. He could always count on it to lift his spirits during the rough patches.

Michael set down the cassette player, removed the headphones from his ears, and reached for his diary. Its black paperback cover was faded, and thin strands of black thread were exposed along the binding. Letters, reflections on imprisonment, and diary entries were the entirety of his to-do list.

His pen had been slowly running out of ink since his very first day in confinement. He hoped that his words wouldn't fade away before someone read them.

One entry read:

The assassinations of Martin Luther King Jr. and Robert Kennedy will surely stand as two defining moments in our country's history. From my "unique" position, I can only read about them in the newspapers. I should be watching the television coverage at home with my family. Who will explain the true meaning of the nation's great loss to my children?

Michael was a model prisoner; he never complained. He even helped the guards resolve some of their own personal problems. One day in November, not that the months meant much to Michael anymore, a guard named Woody perched outside of his cell.

Woody had worked on that particular cellblock for years and had come to know many of the inmates quite well. Although most of them were hardened criminals, Woody sensed that Michael was different.

"Hey Aronstein, what would you do with ten thousand dollars?"

"Probably hire another team of lawyers to work on my next appeal."

"Nah, you know what I mean. What would you invest in? My mom passed away recently and left me a life insurance policy."

"Well," Michael started, with a twinkle in his eyes, "it depends on the amount of risk you're willing to take."

"Okay. Can you be more specific?"

"It's real simple. You can put your money in the bank, where it'll be safe and insured. You'll receive a guaranteed interest on your deposit. Another option is to invest in more speculative ventures, like stocks, from which you could receive dividends as well as profit from the appreciation of the value—if the company performs well. But there are risks," he added.

"Which are?" Woody asked.

"Stocks don't always appreciate in value; they fluctuate. You can lose your money just as quickly as you purchase the stock. You should invest in sound companies, blue chip stocks that have historically demonstrated solid growth. Another alternative is to invest in a good mutual fund. In that case, analysts will do thorough research and invest your money in a pool of companies, rather than one. That limits your downside risk exposure."

"So, basically, it's like I'm gambling in Vegas. Either I can put it all on red right off the bat or spread my chips around to a few different games, make a night out of it."

"Pretty much. But you'll have better odds betting on the market than on the roulette wheel, as long as you do your research."

"Okay, Mike, that makes a lotta sense," Woody responded, shaking his head in amazement. "Good looking out."

Michael watched inmate after inmate take the long march to the electric chair. He knew that it was only a matter of time before his number came up. He marked each passing day on his calendar, wondering who would eventually replace him. He longed for the days on the other side of the prison, when Pete was his neighbor. Back then, he still held out hope that he'd find the light at the end of the tunnel. Now he wondered if he'd made the right decision in opting not to testify on his own behalf. Maybe he should have ignored Andrew's advice and pleaded his case directly to the jury.

Andrew's numerous appeals only prolonged the final curtain. Life had passed Michael by. His mind nearly warped, he was just about ready to give up. Dying in the electric chair would be much easier than lingering on as he was. With the swift flick of a switch, his suffering would be over.

Chapter 34

*L*ife carried on outside of the prison walls, but Michael could only read about it in the newspapers and the few letters he received. Michael's sister Becky got married, but Michael couldn't share in the celebration. All he had was a stack of photographs from the affair.

Terrible news struck in the winter of 1974. Michael's father suffered a sudden heart attack and passed away. Herbie had always been a paragon of good health, so the tragedy came as an even greater shock for the Aronstein family. Michael wished he could have consoled his mother and sister in person, but his request to attend the funeral was denied. Michael mourned his father's death alone in his cell.

Technology progressed in leaps and bounds. The automobile companies cranked out new makes and models. The VCR, a video game called Pong, and Dr. Jarvis's artificial heart all made their debuts. New singing sensations Neil Diamond and Rod Stewart hit the airwaves, and Broadway's marquees announced blockbuster shows such as *Jesus Christ Superstar* and *Les Miserables*. But for Michael, everything seemed to be moving in the opposite direction.

Things also continued to deteriorate for the rest of the Aronstein family. Their abundance of cash had vanished into thin air. Lauren had to borrow money from her parents just to keep up with some of the household bills. Frustration led to constant bickering in the house, as they all felt the weight of struggling to maintain their old lifestyle. New clothes, new shoes, new jewelry; these things that they had previously taken for granted were now a stretch. Even taking family vacations had become a thing of the past. It wasn't easy to make such sacrifices.

The children grew up without a father figure in their lives. Lauren attended back-to-school nights and arranged birthday celebrations on her own in her husband's absence. Michael had pinned pictures of his children up against his cell wall, but they couldn't replace the experience of witnessing the girls mature with his own eyes.

It was heartbreaking to miss Brittney, Abbey, and Julia putting on makeup for the very first time and stumbling down the stairs in high-heeled shoes. Even shaking the hand of Abbey's first date would have been a dream come true.

The bond between Michael and his children slowly diminished; both letters and visits came less and less frequently. Disassociating themselves from their father helped the children escape their reality.

Lauren filed for divorce and attempted to start a new life without Michael. She dated other men, but couldn't bring herself to go to bed with any of them while raising three girls all by herself.

Eventually, she began a relationship with Paul Plankton, an attractive young schoolteacher whom she met at work. Different from Michael in countless ways, Paul brought out emotions within Lauren that had long lied dormant. He was a gentleman, but more importantly, an understanding and caring individual. And he could make her laugh on command.

In addition to a strong attraction, they shared common goals. The children were thrilled that Lauren had found a soul mate to help her regain some happiness in her tangled existence. Although life was getting progressively better for Michael's family, his own was decaying like a rotten apple.

Chapter 35

*I*t's January, 1975. Late January, to be slightly more precise. Some years have passed since the sensational Aronstein trial. Still reclining in my office chair, I notice a familiar face flash on the screen of our newswire service. It's a guy named Casey Malloy, who's being held as a suspect in Mississippi for a string of rapes and homicides.

And he's a dead ringer for Michael Aronstein!

"Hey Ed! You hungry yet?" Peggy had snuck up on me.

"I could sure use an O'Malley's burger," I shout above the sound of my stomach growling. "Plus I never got the chance to fill you in on the Aronstein case."

We head over to our favorite bar across the way. The hostess leads us to a secluded table in the corner and hands over two menus. She reads the daily specials, which are also handwritten on a chalkboard on the wall. I take the cloth napkin from underneath the neatly affixed silverware and place it on my thighs, and Peggy does the same.

I chat with Peggy about some of the stories she's been working on before I mention the intriguing newsflash I had seen earlier.

"So do you remember the details of the case?" I ask her.

"Yeah, I think so. The rich scumbag who cheated on his wife and killed his mistress?"

"Allegedly—he allegedly killed his mistress," I half-jokingly clarify, as she has no clue about the bombshell I'm about to drop.

"No, not allegedly. He was convicted. He's in jail," she affirms.

"That's true, but I just came across an odd newsflash that might make you reconsider your certainty."

"And what was that?" she spouts incredulously.

"A man named Casey Malloy was just arrested in Mississippi for the rape and murder of this gorgeous broad. They're trying to link him to another bunch of unsolved homicides."

"Okay, so there's a potential serial killer in the South. I'm not sure how that relates to Aronstein."

"I saw a picture of the suspect—he's a virtual clone of Michael!"

"You mean this guy could be his twin brother?"

"Exactly."

"So they're both killers," Peggy deduces.

"Maybe not. No one ever mentioned an identical twin in court. That's fishy in itself. Also, I never thought Michael fit the profile of a killer. He emphatically insisted on his innocence, and it always seemed genuine. His attorney advised him to plead guilty and work out a plea bargain, but Aronstein wouldn't hear of it. That shows just how strong his convictions were."

"Even so, he's still an adulterer," Peggy says.

"Yes. That much he admitted. But it doesn't warrant a death sentence," I insist.

"I don't know, Ed. You need more to go on than your gut."

"Whaddya mean?" I latch onto the sides of my bulging abdomen. "Take a look at this."

Right on cue, the waitress returns with my burger. Peggy bursts out in laughter, and we put the issue aside for the moment.

After the meal, we head back to the office, and I immediately dial the sheriff's office in Columbus, Mississippi. An officer tells me that they're aware of the incident, but that the boys down in Macon are handling it. I jot down their office number and the lead detective's name. I call him on his direct line.

"Detective Sweeney here," he answers.

"Detective, glad I could get a hold of you. Let me introduce myself—I'm Edward Cunningham, from the City Press up here in New York."

"That's quite a ways away, Ed. How can I help you?" Sweeney replies.

"I saw a newsflash this afternoon about a prisoner you've got locked up. His name's Casey Malloy."

"Right, we just nabbed the sick bastard. What about him?"

"Well, I covered this high-profile case a few years back, and your prisoner is a clone of the convicted murderer. A man named Michael Aronstein."

"Not sure where you're going with this, Ed."

"Aronstein's been on Death Row for years, but he's never confessed. The guy had never committed a crime in his life. It's never sit quite right with me."

"Lemme see if I got this straight. You have two individuals, over a thousand miles between 'em, who bear a striking resemblance to each other, and are both convicted of murder. Sounds like a classic coincidence," the detective surmises.

"I don't think so. Wait till you see the picture. These guys could be twins and not even know it. Michael never mentioned anything of the sort during the trial. Isn't it possible that he's taking the rap for his twin brother?"

"Sure, it's possible." Sweeney pauses, likely to internally debate whether he should give me the time of day.

"What's Casey's background?" I ask. Another long pause.

"Okay, I've got it right in front of me. Pretty long rap sheet. He's never been accused of murder before, but here's something about an attempted rape."

I silently pump my fist in celebration. Seems like Sweeney's leaning towards my side.

"Ed, why don't you give me your number? I'll call you back after I check into this a little further," he suggests. "Also, send me that picture of Aronstein. I gotta see this bastard."

I give him my number, and sit back in my chair, satisfied, my conscience clear.

Chapter 36

After hanging up with me, Detective Sweeney led Casey Malloy into "the cage," the station's snug interrogation room, equipped with a two-way mirror. The members of the homicide unit let him stew for a few minutes, watching him closely from the other side of the glass.

They already had a solid case; Malloy's fingerprints were plastered all over the bloody knife that was found in a bed of bushes a few blocks from the crime scene. Multiple witnesses picked him out of a lineup with ease and subsequently confirmed that he left a local bar with the victim just an hour before the time of death.

But they still needed a confession—that'd make it a slam-dunk.

Sweeney calmly entered the chamber and took a seat across from Casey, who was shackled to the desk. The detective advised him of his right to an attorney, which Malloy waived without hesitation. A pleasant surprise for a homicide cop.

Sweeney started off slowly.

"Hello Casey, I'm Detective Sweeney," he said, deliberately monotone. He would usually improvise his approach after getting a sense of the perp's willingness to cooperate.

"A pleasure," Malloy hissed. That was all Sweeney needed. He barreled ahead.

"I'll be straight with you, kid. We know you killed that girl, and you damn well know it too. So tell me—and I want you to take a second to think this through—why'd you do it?"

Casey sat up in his chair, barely rattled by the accusation. He stared Sweeney in the eyes and exhaled a foul breath in his direction. It reeked of concrete and metal bars.

"I didn't do nothin'," he said. The jailhouse motto, bad grammar and all.

Sweeney shook his head in disbelief, smirking.

"Have it your way, buddy. It's only a matter of time."

Casey remained stone-faced. Sweeney stood up, utilizing the desk for some leverage. He took a few steps toward the door and turned back to Malloy.

"You ever been to New York City?" he asked.

Casey's eyes widened. Bright, shining full moons. That was enough for Sweeney; he walked out of the cage a newfound believer. In my theory, that is.

Malloy definitely played a role in Maria Salvatez's murder, and Sweeney resolved to prove it. But he didn't call me right away. Instead, he got to work typing up a search warrant for the last known address listed on Casey's record. It was an old boarding house on the other side of town.

He was nearly halfway through the document when a young officer dropped off the envelope I had sent in the mail. Sweeney carefully slit open the top with a department-issued letter opener.

One glance at Michael's photo removed any lingering doubt he might have had. They were identical. Aronstein looked much more put-together, but otherwise, the resemblance was uncanny.

That's when he decided to pick up the phone. Luckily, I'm still hanging around the office, procrastinating my way through the weekly crime report. I'd been unable to focus since we had last spoken.

"Ed, you loony old son-of-a-gun," Sweeney chortles. "You weren't lying. I can't take my eyes off this photo."

"You think there's something to it?"

"Oh yeah. Malloy's involved, alright. You should have seen his mug when I mentioned New York. Eyes opened up like he was starin' down a Mack truck. He's got a story for us, no doubt about that."

"What'd he say?"

"Nothing yet. Still haven't fully broken him. First I'm gonna get this search warrant over to the judge. We'll find something there, where he lays his head. Should take about a week or two."

"A week or TWO?" I exclaim. "We don't have that much time. Michael's scheduled to be executed next week."

"No shit. Why didn't ya say so?"

"Tact, Detective. Tact." Sweeney chuckles. "What would you have said if I called you up, proposed my theory, then insisted that you look into it right away?" I continue.

"I reckon I'd have told you to go screw your neighbor's beagle," Sweeney says.

"What an image. Worthy of the Press," I proclaim.

I'm glad this guy's on my side.

"Alright, I'll see what I can do to expedite the process. I'll ring ya tomorrow either way," the detective promises.

I thank Sweeney and drop the phone onto the receiver. Time to get some rest.

True to his word, the detective calls back the following evening. Something in his voice tells me that he's got good news. He goes on to recount how he called in a favor to a judge with whom he plays poker. The warrant had been executed earlier in the day.

They tore through Malloy's apartment in search of evidence tying him to the recent murder down South. Sweeney supervised the raid, keeping an eye out for anything related to New York or Michael Aronstein. After several fruitless hours of ransacking, an officer stumbled upon a hidden compartment built into the ceiling of Malloy's closet.

Inside they found a musty trench coat and a rumpled pair of women's underwear. Satin, with a pink ribbon, Sweeney gleefully specifies. I let out a squeal, which Sweeney mistakes for a shared interest in the panties.

I explain my excitement and fill him in on the details of the Aronstein case. I had reviewed the reports threefold earlier in the day. Aronstein was wearing a trench coat on the night of the murder. The local cops had found a matching button in Maria's apartment. Sweeney jots that down and makes a note to check if Malloy's coat is missing any.

Maria's rifled-through underwear drawer had seemed irrelevant to New York's Finest at the time, but it's a pertinent piece of evidence now that Malloy's pink satin keepsake has turned up at his apartment.

My seemingly wild speculation is gaining veracity right before my eyes. Or my ears, rather. Sweeney's still on the line.

Preoccupied with concocting a way to rub this all in Peggy's face, I'd forgotten about the jolly detective. I bid him adieu for the night and return my focus to the blank crime report that's perched above my typewriter's roll bar.

Detective Sweeney didn't waste a moment either. He hustled down to the evidence locker and reexamined that trench coat. Turns out I was right. A sprig of loose thread stuck out from the spot usually occupied by the third button below the jacket's collar.

Sweeney bolted down the hallway and into the station's cellblock. He rattled the bars of Casey's cell, waking him from a deep slumber—by prison standards, that is. Malloy came to and groggily cursed him off.

Into his cell went the prison guards, dragging him down the hallway back to the cage. Sweeney followed closely behind.

"Here's the deal, Malloy," Sweeney started. "We just searched your apartment. What do you think we found?"

"A big pile of jack shit."

"Nice try, but you're way off. In fact, what we found is gonna land *you* in a pile a shit, that's for damn sure."

"Yer bluffin," Malloy snapped. Sweeney reached into his back pocket and presented to Casey a worn-in black leather sleeve, shaped like a knife.

Malloy blankly gazed at the damning evidence and let out a reluctant sigh.

"I'll talk," he announced, "but only if you guarantee I won't get the hot seat."

"I can't make that promise without the D.A.'s approval, but I assure you that I'll do what I can. Long as you cooperate."

Casey sat perfectly still, eyes still glazed over, as he mulled over the offer.

"Fine. I'll take that."

Sweeney nodded and promptly left the room. He returned with a tape recorder and switched it on.

"Okay. Start with your name."

"My name's Casey Malloy." He pursed his lips, unsure of where to begin.

"Keep going, stupid. Let's hear it," Sweeney urged him.

Malloy glared at the detective.

"I ain't stupid, pork chop. Lemme collect my thoughts." They sat in silence for a nearly a full minute until Malloy cleared his throat and began.

"I killed that girl. I don't know her name, but I done killed her." Malloy turned back to the detective, expecting him to be satisfied. Sweeney wasn't.

"Elaborate for me, Casey. You know what that means?" Sweeney barked.

Malloy erupted with a growling snort, forcing a wad of mucus up his throat. He spat onto the ground and bolted upright.

"WHADDYA WANNA HEAR, GUY?" Casey thundered. Sweeney leapt to his feet and eyed up the prisoner, ready to restrain him even further if necessary. Malloy just kept jabbering at a high volume.

"THAT I'M A 42 YEAR OLD ORPHAN? THAT I WAS ABANDONED AS A BABY AND RAISED BY SOME PODUNK FARMING FOLK WHO COULDN'T GIVE TWO SHITS ABOUT ME?"

He wasn't quite yelling, but telling his story rather emphatically. Nevertheless, Sweeney kept his guard up.

"I NEVER GOT MY FAIR SHAKE! MY LIFE'S GONE NOWHERE— "

Casey lowered his voice and sank down into his chair.

"Nowhere but—downhill." Sweeney returned to his seat as well. He reclined, gesturing for Casey to continue.

The way Sweeney tells it, Malloy started to ramble on and on like he was on the couch. About how he never felt wanted as a child, and acted out in high school, drinking and smoking. Which led to petty theft, assaults, and the like.

He revealed all the details of the gruesome murder for which he was pinched; per usual, he was celebrating his most recent score with a lascivious woman he found walking the street late at night. Apparently, after their dalliance, she demanded a higher fee than she had originally requested. Casey let loose on her, repeatedly stabbing her in the abdomen with the knife he kept at his right ankle. He claimed it was his first and only murder, that he didn't plan it, and that he was sorry—

"—and blah-blah-blah," Sweeney finishes.

"Wow. What a wackjob. So you've still got nothing on the Aronstein thing?" I ask. Though titillating, his story wasn't what I had hoped to hear.

"The guy was going off the rails. I'm talkin' beyond unstable, Eddie. I'm gonna revisit that one in the morning."

It's 3 AM at this point, and we're both still at work.

"Okay, Detect—wait a minute, what's your first name?"

"You got it," he answered with a chuckle. "Detective."

Chapter 37

*D*espite Sweeney's solid police work, I still have some unanswered questions. To that end, I contact Andrew Fox, Aronstein's attorney and best pal. Fortunately, he takes my call and is willing to chat for a few minutes in between client meetings. I explain my background with the case and bring him up to speed on the latest developments: Casey Malloy, the matching trench coat, the pink underwear.

Though overjoyed to hear about these developments, he curtly confirms that Michael's set to be executed a week from today. Since time is dwindling, I launch right into my probe.

"Does Michael have a twin brother?" I ask.

"No, not that I know of. We've been friends since kindergarten, and he never mentioned anything like that," Andrew responds.

"Okay. Do you know if he is his parents' biological child?"

"Now you might be onto something. Michael once mentioned that he was adopted, but he said it was practically at birth. So theoretically, I guess he could have a twin out there somewhere and not even know it."

"Thanks for your time, Mr. Fox. I'd like to follow up on this with Michael's parents. Do you mind giving me their number?"

"Sure. But it's just Mrs. Aronstein, now. Herbie passed a little while back."

"Sorry to hear that," I offer. "In the meantime, I'll send over a copy of Casey Malloy's mug shot. I'd like to hear what you make of it."

"Excellent. I'll have my secretary give you the address, as well as Mrs. Aronstein's information. Good luck, Ed. Speak to you soon."

Andrew's not quite as colorful a character as Detective Sweeney, but I can tell that he's just as committed to my cause. He clicks a button to put me on hold, and another piece of the puzzle locks into place.

I proceed to contact Sadie Aronstein, hoping to further explore the specifics of Michael's adoption. She picks up after just one ring and cordially agrees to my request for information. I briefly summarize my recent activities and reiterate my wish to exonerate her son.

"Thank you, sir," she says. "We need all the help we can get. The state won't even look at our latest appeal."

"Of course, Mrs. Aronstein. Let's start from the beginning."

"We adopted Michael just a few days after he was born, in July of 1933. The day of his bris—oh, that was the most beautiful day of my life. That's the traditional Jewish ritual of circumcision."

"I'm familiar. After all, I do live in New York."

She chuckled, and continued, "Uncle Ben, Aunt Lily, Mark, David, Sarah—the whole family squeezed into our little apartment to welcome our baby Michael. Herbie, my late husband, and I had been trying for a child for years, to no avail. So when Michael arrived on our doorstep, it seemed like nothing short of a miracle.

I can still picture his tiny little body, barely visible underneath Herbie's father's tallis and yamulke. Rabbi Sakowitz, such a nice young man, spoke so eloquently at the ceremony, detailing the significance of Michael's Hebrew name and why he was named after Herbie's father. It was so beautiful—"

I can tell that she's starting to get choked up, so I chime in.

"That does sound lovely, Mrs. Aronstein. Can you recall the circumstances of the adoption? The agency you used?"

"A neighbor and good friend of ours, Ann Wilson, made all of the arrangements. Her cousin worked for an adoption agency. All we were told was that he was abandoned on a church doorstep somewhere down in Alabama."

"Alabama?" I think of Sweeney, Malloy's similar origins, and a thousand possibilities as to how I could link these two men. "What town?"

"I'm afraid that's all I know," she apologized.

"No problem, that's very helpful," I continue. "How can I reach Ms. Wilson?"

"Oh, I haven't seen Ann in years. Last I'd heard, she moved in with a relative after falling ill. But I suppose I have her contact info written down somewhere. Can you hang on for a moment?"

I affirm that I can, and she starts to rummage for her old address book. After she reads off the address, I cordially thank her for her time and hang up the phone.

Ann Wilson lives out in Yonkers, so I take the short train ride and pay her a visit. She's confined to a wheelchair, but her mind is still sharp as a seamstress's needle.

Seated in her niece's cozy living room, we discuss the Aronstein family and how tragic Michael's fall from grace had been. She fondly recalls the events leading up to his adoption, the details of which I had just heard from Sadie, as well as the day of Michael's bris. She had brought a homemade apple pie—the same recipe as the one I'm currently devouring. I press her for more, but Ann is unable to fill in any more holes.

"All I know is that they found the baby wrapped in a blanket on the steps of an Alabama church. If the janitor hadn't found him--" Ann pauses, not wanting to consider the other possibilities. "Nobody knew who the parents were."

I take a bite of my pie to break the awkward silence. Then I prod a little more.

"How about the name of the adoption agency?"

She stumbles for a moment then blurts out, "The Watchful Eye Adoption Agency."

"Are you sure?" I ask.

"I'm positive," she replies. "I'd tell my cousin Mary all the time how much I loved that moniker. It's comforting, isn't it? Knowing that those poor little babies are being watched over."

To me, the phrase connotes a Big Brother-like paranoia, but I agree anyhow and thank her again for her time.

Back at the office, I crack open the company's immense nationwide directory and find a phone number for Watchful Eye. Fortuitously, the agent who picks up is familiar with Michael's case. Just as I start to rattle off my opening spiel, he stops me dead in my tracks, citing the company's strict confidentiality policy. He says that only a court order would supersede such restrictions.

I'd have to reach out to Sweeney again to obtain one within the short time span I have left. I know he's reliable, but he's already cashed in a big favor for me. It might be too soon to ask him for another.

As an investigative reporter, I've accumulated a slew of creative ways to get past a seemingly dead end. Visiting the library is at the top of the list. I locate the newspaper records from Alabama in July of 1933 and pore through issue after issue until my hands are stained an inky black. Then I hit pay dirt: a headline in the *Sulligent Standard* from July 13th,1933.

Baby Boy Abandoned on the Doorstep of a Church.

That was Michael. One down, one more to go. I still have to find an item that places Casey's abandonment right around the same time. After scrutinizing every column of the *Standard* to no avail, I move on to the surrounding areas. Birmingham, Tuscaloosa, Jasper—still nothing. Next I venture into Mississippi; Sulligent's right on the border. Sure enough, the first publication I pick up, the *Columbus Dispatch*, has an eerily similar headline on the front page of the Local section, on the same day as the issue of the *Standard* I'd found.

Baby Boy Abandoned in a Local Hospital Stairwell.

Back in the thirties, the authorities likely didn't have the resources or the motivation to discover the link between the two cases. But now I'm on the job.

I contact the hospital and explain the dire circumstances, stressing that it's time-sensitive. The security guard I speak with, a kindly compassionate old man, locates the old files stored in the basement. He must be violating protocol, though he doesn't say a word about it. The internal document confirms the account from the *Dispatch* and goes on to identify the eventual adopter: a staff nurse named Mary Jo Malloy. I've long been unjustifiably confident in my hunch, but this little nugget is the proof that could save Aronstein's life.

The guard is kind enough to give me Mary Jo's last known contact information. That's when my incredible luck runs out; the Malloys had long since moved from that residence and hadn't left a forwarding address. The phone company confirms that the line has been disconnected for nearly a decade.

Soldiering on, I delve into Casey Malloy's criminal record, which Sweeney had dictated to me over the phone. The best lead I can find is his former parole officer. I contact the parole board in search of another helpful citizen. I leave a message with the night receptionist and return home after a long day.

Sure enough, the following afternoon, Malloy's parole officer gives me a ring. He knows practically everything about the sicko and doesn't spare a detail. Casey's troubles dated back as far as grade school, when he was suspended and expelled for touching girls in inappropriate places. His adoptive parents, the Malloys, had a good reputation amongst their neighbors until Casey began to stir up trouble. His rap sheet grew larger and larger through the years, but after serving a few stints at county, Casey was released back into the world.

When I share my suspicions with the officer, he doesn't hesitate to agree that Malloy is capable of such a crime. Unfortunately, that's all he can tell me. He hasn't seen Casey in years.

Undaunted, I search high and low for any imaginable clue that would bring me closer to the truth. I spend hours scouring through records and contacting doctors who may have delivered a set of twins, but I can't gain any traction.

That is, until I reconsider the fact that baby Michael was dropped off at a church in Alabama. The abandoner must have lived locally, or perhaps even belonged to the congregation. I consult the telltale *Standard* article and jot down the name of the church. Father McKenna, the current leader of the parish, is familiar with the incident, as he had been serving as a young apprentice at the same church back in the early thirties. In light of magnitude of the situation at hand, he agrees to do his part to save an innocent life. Though he says that he can't discuss anything over the phone.

I dart to the airport and catch the first flight out. No use in holding back now. I'm already in pretty deep. Father McKenna graciously picks me up from the airport and takes me to a decent motel. During the ride, he discloses that a congregant had made a unique confession many years back. Under the cloth's strict code of ethics, he couldn't take any legal action at the time, nor could he divulge the person's name to me today.

However, he throws me a bone, providing the name of an acquaintance of the churchgoer in question: Nelly Mulligan. He doesn't elaborate on the nature of her relationship with the congregant who had made the pertinent confession, but he does tell me that Nelly lives practically a stone's throw away from the church. A devoted Catholic, she still attends every single Sunday Mass despite her advanced age.

I find a phone booth nearby and locate her phone number in the directory that sits underneath the handset. A young woman named Emma answers the phone and goes on to explain that she is Nelly's niece. And that she's also served as her aunt's caretaker since she had fallen ill a few months earlier.

Something about my query must have struck a chord, since Emma pauses for a brief moment after hearing about my interest in abandoned twin boys. She agrees to share some pertinent information with me, but only in person.

In what seems like an instant, I'm on her front porch, knocking on her door. The second she creaks open the door and

I get a look at her soft blue eyes, I know that she's Michael's mother. There's no doubt about it. I'm onto something really big.

Emma invites me in with a warm greeting and offers me a beverage, as well as an armchair in her cozy living room. Though reluctant to discuss the case at first, she begins to open up as the conversation progresses.

She starts off by telling me that she is most likely the mother of both Michael Aronstein and Casey Malloy, and then launches into her story:

———————————————————————————

Chapter 38

*I*t was a warm Sunday afternoon in the spring of 1932. I headed into town, dressed in my nicest plaid skirt, with a ponytail down to my waist. I had worn my hair like that for an entire week as I waited for my misplaced hairbrush to turn up. But since my hair was getting kinda natty, I gave up on finding the brush and took a walk to the general store to purchase a new one.

I entered to the jingling sound of the wind chimes that hung on the door and saw this handsome guy with dirty blonde hair and blue eyes kneeling down to the floor. He instinctively looked up and met my gaze, nearly dropping the supplies he was holding.

I was still pretty shy at that age, so I coyly turned in the other direction and walked down the grocery aisle, even though I had just gone shopping with my mama the day before. I remember my entire body was electrified. I'd never felt like that before.

After pretending to examine a bag of flour, I located the hairbrushes and took one up to the counter. Wouldn't ya know it, that boy was in the middle of paying for his goods. He was busy chatting with Earl, the store's owner, so he didn't notice me behind him. I just lingered nearby, close enough to hear their conversation.

"So Billy, how's your family doin'?" inquired Earl. "Haven't seen your dad 'round here lately."

"They're doin' just fine. Pop's been workin' hard, try'na pick as much cotton as he can before winter sets in." Billy responded.

"Yeah, a lot of the farmers around town are complainin' about the prices they're fetchin' for crops."

"This depression sure put quite a hurtin' on a lot of us."

"And on me too, y'know. So—anything else I can getcha?" Earl snickered.

"Some of yer finest chewin' tobacco should do it." The elderly shop keep reached underneath the counter and grabbed a thick pouch of the brown leaves.

"Your family goin' to the square dance next weekend?" he asked Billy.

"Yeah, we'll be there. N'fact I'm bout to stop next door for a haircut. Gotta look my best."

"Well yer in good hands with Sammy. Fixed me up real nice just the other day." Earl removed his hat to reveal freshly cut locks. *"I'll see you next Saturday, then. Tell your folks I said hello."*

Billy signed for his merchandise and walked towards the exit. But as I laid my brush down on the counter, he turned back to steal another glance at me. Gosh, my face must've been red as a cherry.

Our eyes met again for a short moment, and this time we exchanged smiles. He gave me a slight parting wave of his hand, probably hoping that I'd return the nice gesture.

But I was frozen, I tell ya, just paralyzed with fear. His face dropped when I didn't respond, and he ambled out of the store right quick.

After I paid for my brush, I walked outside and made a left towards Samson's Barbershop. I just had to get one last look at that boy. I crept up alongside the wall and peered through the *glass. There he was, in the chair closest to the front of the shop. That was the moment I decided to take up square dancing. I had to see that boy again.*

The next Saturday evening, excitement filled the air at the corral. The annual square dance was the biggest social function in town. Cars and pickup trucks were strewn on all over the fields surrounding the old barn.

Although most people got all dressed up in cowboy attire for a long night of dancin', I was only there to see Billy.

From the large entryway, I watched a large group of couples swinging each other to and fro in the center of the floor. All the laughter, clapping, and clip-clopping of cowboy boots nearly drowned out the melodious sounds of the band, which was made up of a banjo, accordion, violin, and guitar.

I scanned the faces of the raucous dancers, as well as those of others who huddled on the sideline to watch. But I couldn't find Billy.

Of course, the moment I stopped looking for him, he walked right by me. My heart rate noticeably accelerated, and a lump formed in my throat. He was so handsome; I couldn't take my eyes off him.

He must have sensed that I was staring at him, because after taking about ten paces, he looked up and met my gaze. To my delight, he was beaming. Without any hesitation, he ran back across the dance floor and extended his arms as an invitation to dance. I graciously hooked my elbow to his and joined him as the tune came to a climactic end. Like a true gentleman, he removed his hat and bowed to me. I reciprocated with a curtsy.

"So I guess you remember me, then," he joked.

"Yes, I do. The general store, right?" I feigned a bit of uncertainty, too bashful to admit to my budding obsession.

"That's right," he affirmed. *"By the way, my name's Billy. Billy Hudson."* He extended his hand for a shake.

"Pleasure to meet you, Billy. I'm Emma Blackstone."

"And same to you. So what part of town are you from?"

"Vernon"

"About six miles north of here?" Billy surmised.

"Yeah, about that, I think,"

"You must be close to all the shopping." He paused, then continued, *"Ya know, I don't live too far from there myself."*

The band launched into another song, interrupting the slight lull in our conversation. The bandleader announced that next one was ladies' choice.

"How about another dance?" I asked Billy, unconsciously twirling my hair.

"Why, I'd be downright dee-lighted to, Miss Blackstone," he said in an exaggerated Southern drawl.

We swayed to a slow Western ballad, holding each other tightly and enjoying the warmth that grew between us in those few minutes. When the song ended, we both knew that something magical had happened. The mutual attraction was palpable, to say the least. We left the dance floor for the refreshment stand, where he purchased two soft drinks.

"Excuse me for asking, but how old are you, Emma?" Billy inquired.

"I'm sixteen," I said.

"What's that, eleventh grade?"

"Yes, indeed," I confirmed.

"What school do you go to?"

"Jackson High," I answered with a smile. *"What's with all these questions? Tell me somethin' about your own self."*

"Well I'm seventeen," Billy replied. "But I'm not in school anymore. I had to drop out to help my folks with the farm. With the Depression an' all, they can't afford to pay all the workers we'd need to keep things running smoothly."

Looking to extend the conversation, he continued, "What do you want to be when you get out of school?"

"My mom said she could get me a good payin' job at the mill if I finished up."

I had barely gotten the last word out when a girl's hand latched onto Billy's arm. It was Mary Jo, one of his younger sisters.

"Mom's been lookin' all over for you. We have to leave—Tommy ain't feelin' so hot."

"Ok, I'll be right there." he assured her.

She ran off to join her mother, and Billy turned back to me.

"I'm sorry, I gotta go. My little brother's got polio, so sometimes he—"

"I understand. You go ahead. It was nice to see you again---and meet you for the first time, I guess."

"Likewise. Until next time, darlin'." He took my hand and gracefully pressed his lips to the skin just above my knuckles--the perfect spot.

Then he was gone. And with all the commotion, he had forgotten to ask how to contact me in the future.

Chapter 39

A *couple of weeks passed by and I had finally begun to forget about Billy, my mysterious prince. Then one day after school let out, I was walking towards town with some of my classmates, like I usually did. One by one, they all went their separate ways, and I continued on my own. That's when I heard the clunking of an automobile slowly creeping up behind me.*

"Need a ride?" the driver shouted, as he pulled up to the pavement.

I kept walking without responding, as Mama always told me to be wary of strange men offering a ride. He crawled along in his truck and called out, "Wanna go to the square dance?"

That drew my attention. I turned to see Billy behind the wheel. I approached the truck to and stuck my head inside the passenger side window.

"Remember me?" Billy asked, leaning over. Though he must've been able to tell that I had.

"Oh yeah, we danced together at the corral last month."

"Hop on in. I'll take you home." I opened the door and entered the vehicle.

"Where in these parts do you live?"

"In the countryside. Not too far from the edge of town. I'll show you,"

"Who was that guy you were walking with?" he asked.

"Just an old friend." I blushed, sensing Billy's budding jealousy. He sighed, relieved that he didn't have any competition.

"How did you know where I went to school?" I asked.

"You told me at the dance. When we got sodas."

"Oh, that's right."

We drove through the scenic countryside, past the vast amounts of flat farmland, until we reached my house, which was nestled on an acre of land surrounded by wild grass. It was a small, modest home, resembling a bungalow or wood shack, but spacious enough for my mama and me. Though she had to work a lot of shifts at the mill just to maintain our poor and simple lifestyle.

As we pulled into the dirt driveway, I turned to Billy and thanked him for the ride.

"You're very welcome," he cordially replied.

When I exited the truck and turned to leave, he blurted out, "By the way, there's a new movie, Horse Feathers, *playing in town this weekend. How'd ya like to see it with me Saturday night?"*

"I'd love to. About what time?"

"Around 7:30," he suggested.

"You got a date!"

I walked towards my house, clutching my schoolbooks tightly, unable to contain my excitement.

Before I knew it, Saturday arrived and Billy walked up to my doorstep at 7:30 on the dot. He must've wanted to make a good first impression, cause he brought a beautiful bouquet of flowers.

My mother greeted him at the door. She was tall and slender, and had her sandy blonde hair pulled back into a bun. I remember she was wearing a plain floral print housedress that day. I owned one just like it.

"Come on in," Mama said.

"Much obliged, Mrs. Blackstone. I'm Billy Hudson."

"Please, call me Doris, honey."

"You must be that boy Emma's been talking about. I hear you're quite the dancer."

"I don't know about that, but I do my darn'dest," he said with a grin.

"Where are you two goin' tonight?" she inquired, her tone conveying a touch of suspicion.

"To the movie theater. There's a new—"

"I hope y'all have a great time. Long as Emma's back by her curfew—the stroke of midnight."

"Of course, Doris, I guarant—"

He trailed off once I entered the room, dressed in tight blue jeans and a tightly fitted top that accentuated my chest. I made sure I looked good for him that night.

"You look great," he said, presenting the bouquet of flowers.

"They're beautiful. Thank you, Billy." I graciously accepted the arrangement and handed it off to Mama.

"Bye, Mama," I yelled.

"Bye. Have a great time!" We joined arms, just like we had at the square dance, and got into his truck. After parking by the theater, Billy went ahead to purchase tickets and a popcorn at the window. The theater was nearly full, but we were still able to claim two open seats off to the right side in the back.

Just as the lights dimmed, Billy' arm brushed up against mine. He took my hand in his and clutched it tightly. It was the first physical contact we'd had since the dance, and he didn't let go all night. We both enjoyed the picture, but couldn't help but gaze at each other from time to time.

After the movie, we went across the street to Wally's drugstore, which served ice cream and fountain soda at the counter. I ordered a vanilla milkshake, extra thick, and Billy asked for a banana split. We shared our desserts, talking and laughing as if we had known each other for years. It was nearly 11:30 when I realized I had to get home to keep my curfew. I had such a fantastic night and didn't want my mother's scolding to ruin it.

Billy pulled into our dirt driveway, cut the ignition, and turned to me.

"I hope you had a good time tonight," he said.

"It was wonderful," I replied with the utmost sincerity.

We looked into each other's eyes and embraced with a passionate kiss. Billy wrapped his arms around my shoulders. He pulled me closer to him so that he could feel the warmth of my body. But I pulled away. It was already a few minutes past my curfew.

"Can we do this again sometime?"

"Yes, indeedy" I replied. I couldn't believe that word came out of my mouth.

"Then I'll be seein' ya soon," he assured me.

Chapter 40

espite Billy's promise, a few more weeks went by without any contact. I spent nearly every free moment sitting by the phone, anxiously waiting to hear from him. Finally, I sucked up my pride and decided to act on my feelings. I looked up his number in the directory and rang his home.

"Hello!" his sister answered.

"Is Billy there?"

"Who is this?"

"Emma Blackstone."

"Ohhhh, I know you," she giggled as she set down the receiver. "Emma Blackstone for you, Billy."

There was a pause and Billy picked up the phone, seemingly out of breath. I could hear his sister in the background whispering, "Is that the girl from the square dance?

"Hello," Billy answered.

"Is that really you?" I asked.

"Yeah, it's me. I'm sorry I haven't called, ya see—"

"How have you been? Are you alright?" I was so nervous; I couldn't stop talking.

"I'm fine."

"I've missed you terribly."

"I miss you too, Emma."

"You haven't called me in weeks. What did I do wrong? Is it someone else?"

"No! Absolutely not," Billy insisted. "I'm sorry I haven't had a chance to reach you. It's been a little crazy around here since my little brother checked into the hospital. I got stuck with all of the chores cause my mom is with Tommy all the time."

"Oh, I'm so sorry to hear that. I hope he's okay." I responded in a consolatory manner, feeling a little selfish for accosting him like that.

"Can I see you again?" he asked, hoping to rekindle the relationship.

"Yes, of course," I responded. "I have a terrific idea. Why don't you come over to my house on Saturday afternoon? I'll have a special surprise for you."

"Okay, that's great! I'll see you then."

"I can't wait," I said.

Thankfully, since my surprise was contingent on fair weather, that next Saturday was a crystal clear day, without a cloud in the sky. Billy pulled his truck up to my house, muffling the sounds of nature that echoed throughout the hollowing trees.

While I packed up the last of the supplies in the kitchen, I overheard the conversation he had with Mama in the front yard.

"Haven't seen you around lately, Billy. How's everything doin'?"

"I've been dealin' with some family problems, but that'll pass."

"Let me call Emma and tell her you're here." I beat her to opening the door, popped my head out, and motioned for Billy to come inside. As soon as it shut behind him, I lunged at him. He lifted both my legs in the air and greeted me with a hug and a big ol' kiss.

221

"What's in the basket?" he asked, as he set me down.

"That's a surprise. Why don't you carry it, and I'll take the blanket?" I suggested.

Billy picked up the basket while I folded the blanket in my arms.

As we left the house, my mother shouted from a stooped position, "Emma! Where ya'll off to?"

"On a picnic"

"Whereabouts?"

"Over by Spring Pond, you know, the old place I used to go fishin' when I was a kid."

"Oh, that's just dandy. Have a good time," she said, waving goodbye.

We drove about a half hour through the countryside and arrived at a remote and desolate area. There wasn't a soul within a ten-mile radius.

"We're here!" I shouted.

We came to a sign posted on a pine tree, which read: Dangerous Water- Contaminated- Do Not Trespass, *but ignored its warning and walked a couple of yards into a densely shaded forest.*

Billy looked puzzled; he must've been wondering what was so special about this place. Nevertheless, he followed me, like a dog and his master, confident that I knew where I was going.

Before we knew it, we stood before a serene, picturesque pond. As a little girl, I used to fish in that isolated paradise. Although the pond had changed a bit—by then it was a murky green color—returning there brought back fond memories of my daddy.

The grassy knoll was as soft as I remembered. It surrounded the entire pond and extended to a dense thicket of pine trees.

Sunlight reflected off the water's surface, where tiny sprinkles of green algae floated amongst a swarm of mosquitoes. It was quiet and peaceful, the perfect place to be alone with Billy, I thought.

We searched for a sunny spot on the low grass, eventually settling on a site around twenty feet from the water's edge. I spread the blanket on the ground, and Billy set the basket on top.

"Let's take a walk," I suggested.

I took my shoes off and led Billy by the hand. We strolled towards the edge of the pond, where I sat down, rolled up the legs of my pants, and splashed my feet in the mucky water.

I arched my back, extended both of my arms, and tilted my head back to gaze at the crystal clear blue sky. Inhaling the crisp air and instantly transported me back to the innocent days of my youth. Though instead of my father, Billy sat beside me, just staring, admiring my beauty as if he were the luckiest man on the planet.

"I remember coming here as a kid," I softly uttered. "Everybody brought their fishin' poles. We caught catfish and watched tadpoles and frogs leapin', with little baby turtles swarming all around. There were at least ten kids fishin' here all the time. I started coming when I was just two," I reminisced.

"Did you come with your mom and dad?"

"Just my daddy. He brought me here a couple of times when I was little." I studied Billy's face. "You know, you kinda remind me of him."

"Where is he now?"

"He was killed in a lumber mill accident. My mom was never the same after that. I always wanted to come back here, but no one would ever take me. You ever go fishin', Billy?"

"Once in a while over at Sulligent Lake. But my dad used to take me quail hunting from time to time."

"Did you ever shoot one down?"

"No, I was too young to handle the rifle. It was too darn heavy."

I laughed. "Do you still go hunting?"

"I would love to, but lately I can't seem to find the time with all the work to do on the farm."

I looked up at the sky. "Look over there!" I exclaimed, pointing to a flock of pelicans. I was amazed at the army of white birds squawking and flapping their wings as they softly glided into the pond. Billy was mesmerized, as well. We sat for a while and captured the marvelous sights, sounds, and smells of nature.

"Too many mosquitoes around here," I complained. "I'm getting hungry anyway. Let's get back to our spot."

We held hands as we returned to the blanket. I opened the picnic basket, excited to unveil the food I prepared for Billy.

"Well, what are we eating?" he asked.

"We'll start with this fresh bread. I just baked it last night. We can dip it in butter, then we'll drink a little bit of whiskey I stole from my mother, long as you promise not to tell."

"Course not," he affirmed.

Billy removed the loaf from the basket and cut off two pieces of bread. I picked up the whiskey bottle, but had some difficulty removing the cork.

"Can you help me with this?" I asked. Billy popped the cork and poured some whiskey for us.

"So tell me," I asked "how many kids you think you'll have when you get married?"

"Never thought about it," he admitted.

"Just take a guess."

"Well, maybe two."

"Why two?"

"Cause I come from a pretty big family. I got a brother and two sisters, and it's a hassle sharing bathrooms and all that stuff."

"Was that your sister I met at the square dance?"

"Yeah, one of 'em. Mary Jo, I think it was."

"How old is she?"

"11"

"She's cute. I could see the resemblance"

"Yeah, but don't be fooled. She can be a pain in the butt sometimes."

I smiled, then continued, "What's it like in your house? I mean living with them every day."

"My two sisters are always fightin', but we're all sympathetic to my little brother Tommy. Me, I'm just a mellow type of guy. Nobody really bothers me. How about you, Emma? How many children are you plannin' to have?"

I hesitated for a moment, then revealed, "I'd like to have a big family. It's kind of lonely at my house with just Mama and me. We're constantly arguing about stupid little things, same as your sisters, and I wouldn't want that in my married life. Plus, I get blamed for everything, since I'm the only other person in the house." Billy laughed.

"What's so funny?" I asked.

"Just thinkin' about the times I got a scoldin' for things my little brother did." Billy turned to the picnic basket. "What's next?" he inquired. I reached my hand deep into the basket to retrieve the remainder.

"I made some fried chicken sandwiches on cornbread, with some fixins."

"Mm-mmm, I reckon I'll try some of that."

We finished off our sandwiches, and I handed Billy a cloth napkin. He wiped the excess food around his mouth and chin, *but didn't get it all. I giggled and dabbed my napkin at the area he missed. We lied down on the blanket, and Billy cradled me under his arm.*

"Did I ever tell you how beautiful you are?" he whispered.

"Did I ever mention how handsome you are?" I countered.

He kissed my lips and pulled my body closer. I spread my lips and extended my tongue into his mouth. We French-kissed until Billy pulled away and looked into my eyes for a moment. He held and caressed my face in his hands as he kissed my forehead, eyes, and cheeks.

He rolled on top of me and we resumed our passionate kissing. He touched every part of my body; I didn't resist at all. Soon enough, we were stark naked. I felt his manhood enter my body, and we were both transported to another stratosphere. Every part of his warm body pressed against mine, and I nearly winced along with each of his powerful thrusts.

"I love you," he whispered in my ear.

"I love you too!" I exclaimed, overcome with emotion.

Suddenly, Billy climaxed, screaming as he released entered my body. I moaned, more than satisfied with my first sexual experience.

We lied next to each other for a few minutes to gain our composure. The sun had already started to recede, so we got dressed and packed up the picnic belongings while we could still see.

I couldn't take my eyes off Billy during the ride home. I thought about how much my life was about to change. We were truly falling in love.

Chapter 41

For the next few months, Billy devoted all his free time to me. He found it difficult to juggle his new responsibilities, with Tommy's moving back and forth from the hospital each week, but he made it work. Billy and I were perfectly happy to share life's simple things together.

Two months after we made love at the pond, I began to perceive a change in my body and feared that I might be pregnant. I confirmed my suspicions on a secret visit to my family doctor. I stayed up at nights thinking about how to handle the problem.

A barrage of questions ran through my mind. How did I ever get myself into this mess? How could I tell my mother? How would she react? What will Billy say? Will he stay with me? Will he marry me? Or should I just run away?

I decided to divulge my secret one evening in November of 1932. My mother was sitting on her rocking chair, reading a book and enjoying the music on the radio. I sat on the side of my bed, trembling, with knots in my stomach. I had thought long and hard about this moment. I slowly entered the family room and positioned myself on the floor in front of the rocking chair. I crossed my legs and folded my arms, unsure of how to break the news.

"Mama, I got something to tell you," I began.

She set down her book, removed her reading glasses, and gave me her full attention.

"I don't know the best way to say this, but I'm pregnant."

"You. Are. WHAT?" In a rage, she rose from the chair. "How did this happen?" she shouted. "Is it that Billy boy?"

"Yes, it's Billy," I sobbed.

My mother continued, "I should have known better. I should have stopped this a long time ago. He's been snoopin' around here too much. I must be blind, or just downright stupid."

She paused and bowed her head, thinking of how to proceed.

"I forbid you from seeing him," my mother commanded. "He'll never step one foot inside this house again! Don't contact him in any way!"

I nodded, as tears streamed from my eyes. "But I love him, Mama!"

"I don't care!" she snapped. "You should be ashamed of yourself. You were supposed to finish up school and get your diploma so you could get a good payin' job."

She paused, and tears began to fill her eyes as well.

"You could've gotten a job in town so we could finally get out of this rat hole," she blubbered. "I wanted you to have a better life than mine! Do you want to struggle like I did for the rest of your life? What's wrong with you, for God's sake?" she shouted.

When Mama finally regained her composure for a brief moment, she commanded, "Emma, I don't want even one soul to know you're pregnant. You'll have to drop out of school and live with Aunt Nelly in Montgomery until the baby comes."

"People are gonna find out, Mama. I'm gonna be raisin' it, right?" I asked.

"That is for me to decide."

"But it's Billy's baby too," I cried out.

I ran to my room, crying and shaking uncontrollably. I just had to speak to Billy, in spite of Mama's orders. There was no time to waste.

The next day, I borrowed Mama's car and drove into town. I would have driven to Billy's home, but I didn't know where he lived. Only his phone number. I headed to the pay phone at the general store and dialed the Hudsons' number.

"Hudson residence," said a voice that must've been Billy's mother's.

"Hello, is Billy there?"

"Who's calling?" she asked.

"It's Emma, Emma Blackstone."

"Oh, hello Emma! I've heard so much about you. Hold on, let me see if he's back from the fields yet."

She called out for Billy, but there was no response.

"Suppose I have him call you back, dear?"

"Okay," I responded. hanging up with disappointment.

The next day Mama helped me pack up my belongings and drove me out to Aunt Nelly's house on the western edge of Alabama. As we drove through downtown Vernon, I gazed out the window at the movie theater and drugstore where Billy and I shared our first date. Tears streamed from my eyes; those fond memories were too difficult to bear.

"Emma, my dear," my mother said. "When I was your age, I fell in love with your father. I wanted so much to go to bed with him, but my conscience wouldn't allow it. I can feel your pain." She tried to sympathize with me.

"I was a virgin until my wedding night. Your father respected my beliefs. I wanted you to follow in my footsteps

and abide by those principles. That's why I raised you how I did. And why I got so upset. I'm so sorry," she said, as tears welled in her eyes.

"It's not that I dislike Billy, but you are just too young and immature to raise a family. I know that deep down you'll find a place in your heart to forgive me."

I processed her words, but remained angry. We sat in silence for the remainder of the trip My thoughts churned—there had to be a way to right this wrong, to turn this nightmare into a happy ending.

After traveling for an hour, we finally reached Aunt Nelly's house and unloaded the baggage. Confined there for the next several months, with only my aunt, I grew depressed. I had very little contact with the outside world. Moreover, Billy never responded to the letter I sent him.

My mother and Aunt Nelly closely examined all of the mail sent from and delivered to the house. Not until years later, after Mama passed, did I find Billy's reply. She had kept it locked up in a drawer at the bottom of her armoire. It read:

My beloved Emma,

I have been trying in vain to get in touch with you. I tried you by phone, but your mother demanded that I stay out of your life and forbid me from seeing you ever again. I'm not sure what I did wrong. If I've hurt you or your mother in any way, I truly apologize.

I've cherished our relationship since it began, and I cannot stop thinking of all the good times we shared. Please respond as soon as you receive this letter. I miss you terribly.

Love always,

Billy

At the time, having been imprisoned at Aunt Nelly's for nearly eight months, I had assumed that Billy just forgot that I existed. My emotions were swirling out of control, and my stomach grew larger and larger.

I reclined on the sofa and shuffled through the pages of a newspaper left over from the night before. In the obituary section, one entry caught my eye. It said that Tommy Hudson of Vernon, Alabama had succumbed to polio at only 8 years old.

I was shocked, saddened, and titillated in a strange way, since it brought back memories of Billy. I wondered how I could get to the funeral; I had to attend that service, no matter what.

Luckily, Aunt Nelly wasn't home on the day of the funeral. I went to the cupboard where she stored some money and, without any hesitation, stole enough cash to cover a taxi ride. With my aunt gone for the day, I had plenty of time to pay my respects and return home without being detected.

I blended in with the other attendees, watching in silence as Tommy's casket rested on a platform above the tiny grave. The priest celebrated Tommy's short life and said a few prayers, including one that began, "Ashes to ashes, dust to dust." Everyone joined in unison to recite the final prayer, a verse from the 23rd psalm entitled, "The Lord is My Shepherd".

Upon completion of the prayer, the crowd parted at the middle to make way for the Hudson family to slowly march to the hearse. I pushed my way up to the front of the crowd and locked eyes with Billy. I remember his face lighting up for a brief moment, until he spotted my bulging stomach. From the look in his eyes, I could tell that he now understood why our relationship had suddenly ended so abruptly. In that instant, the flames inside both of us reignited.

I knew that he desperately wanted to talk to me, but that he recognized that it wasn't the right time or place. I was tempted to join the Hudsons at their home after the funeral, but I couldn't risk arriving home after Aunt Nelly had returned.

My last chance to reunite with Billy had seemingly faded in the wind.

Unfortunately, I couldn't talk to anyone about my feelings. I knew Aunt Nelly would run straight to Mama if she found out that I'd seen Billy.

Then, on the evening of July 12th, 1933, she started pryin'.

"Emma, what do you plan on doing with your life after the baby is born?"

"First, I'd like to finish up high school and get my diploma."

"Then what will you do, dear?"

"I never really thought about it, Aunt Nelly. Maybe get a good typing job?"

"If you can get that, you can advance and eventually become a supervisor. You'll really make a whole lot of money for your family," Nelly added. I couldn't help but recall Billy's and my conversation that day at the pond.

"Can I ask you something? What was it like growing up with my mama?"

"Oh, we would fight about the stupidest things, mostly girly stuff. But that ended soon as your dad came into the picture."

"Why's that?"

"She started spending all her time with him, so she wasn't at home to fight with me."

We shared a laugh, and Aunt Nelly saw it as an opening to pry even further.

"Do you still have feelings for that Billy boy?"

I rolled my eyes and grinned, giving away my answer.

"Very much so," I stated.

Feeling discomfort, I stood up. I looked down at a spot on the sofa and discovered a shallow puddle—my water bag had broken. I didn't know what to do; anxiety set in.

"Oh my god!" Aunt Nelly screamed. "Just sit tight, I'll take care of everything," she assured me. Aunt Nelly ran to the phone and called my mama.

"Doris, it's Nelly. You better get over here right away," she shouted with excitement.

"Is everything alright?"

"Emma broke her bag. The water's flowin' out like a fountain."

"Okay, I'll be there in an hour or so. Did you call your friend, the midwife?"

"I will just as soon as we hang up."

My Aunt Nelly contacted her friend and relayed the information. I lied down in my room. In addition to the emotional trauma, I was also experiencing physical discomfort. My Aunt Nelly grabbed her stopwatch and determined that my contractions were coming in seven-minute intervals. That meant there wasn't too much time left.

I lied there in pain until the midwife appeared at the door with towels, sheets, and extra pillows. She took command of the operation as a navy captain mans the ship.

"Get me some pails of warm water," she ordered. "I'll also need a few more pillows." Aunt Nelly followed her strict instructions and fetched the supplies.

"Don't you fret," the midwife whispered. *"Everything's gonna be just fine."*

My contractions increased in frequency, until they began to come in two-minute intervals. Cold, damp towels covered my head and face, easing my perspiration. My mother arrived and joined Aunt Nelly by my side, holding my hands real tight.

"Spread your legs, Emma!" the midwife yelled.

I vaguely remember screaming *"Mama, Mama!"* amidst excruciating pain.

The contractions sped up; they were now coming each minute. The midwife bent down to examine me.

"There's the head," she shouted. *"Push, goddamn it! Push!"*

I squeezed my eyes tight and gave one last push. The baby boy fell into the midwife's awaiting arms, and his scream amplified the room. She placed the baby on top of my belly and proceeded to clean me up. I was still in excruciating pain.

Suddenly, she spotted another head poking out from between my legs. *"Oh my Lord, she's having twins!"* she exclaimed. Delirious, I bellowed at the top of my lungs.

"Honey, one more time, just one more time, we need you to push," the midwife cried.

With what seemed like my last dying breath, I closed my eyes, clenched my teeth, and pushed as hard as I could. In that moment, I gave birth to another baby boy.

Though something seemed wrong with this child. He didn't start crying right away. I held them both against my chest--and that's the last moment I can recollect from that day.

I awoke the next morning, still incredibly groggy yet eager to see my newborn babies. I had nearly recovered from the pain, and my only desire was to hold them in my arms again.

"Mama, are you there?"

"Yes, Emma. I'm coming. Are you okay?"

"I feel like the wind's been knocked out of me."

"Here dear, drink some of this."

"What is it?"

"Oh, just some mixed vegetable concoction your Granny made for me when I had you. You're gonna need it to regain your strength after that ordeal."

"How are the babies? I want to see them."

"Hush up and drink this. It's good for the soul."

"Where are my babies, Mama?"

"Don't worry about them. They're in good hands now."

"Mama, what do you mean?" I stared at her in disbelief.

I knew from her silence what she had done. She'd gone and broken my heart.

I could feel her pain and by now was ready to head back to my office to report my findings to Andrew. But, before I could even lift myself out of the chair, she began to recant the story about what really occurred on that night after she delivered. It was told to her in later years by Aunt Nelly who got it from her mother and revealed to her in secrecy before she died.

While Emma slept, her mother gathered boxes and blankets to transport the newborns. At 2 AM, she tiptoed through the house, loaded the boys into her makeshift cribs, and placed them in the backseat of her car. It was pitch black outside. There wasn't another vehicle for miles. Doris put the car in reverse and sped off into the darkness. She dimmed her lights and cautiously turned into the parking lot of the community church. After taking a quick look around to ensure that the coast was clear, she snatched one of the boxes and placed it on the church steps.

Doris got back in her car and continued driving towards the state border. Soon she entered Mississippi. She continued on the highway for about a half an hour until she arrived in the town of Columbus. Doris glanced at her rearview mirror and, to her surprise, noticed the flashing lights of a police car. She quickly moved her vehicle to the shoulder to allow the officer to pass, but the vehicle just crept up behind her and motioned for her to pull over. The officer approached her car as Doris rolled down her window.

"Can I see your license and registration card?" he asked.

"Of course, Officer, but what did I do wrong?"

"You're drivin' around without headlights on."

"Oh my God! I am so sorry, Officer."

"Things like this happen, ma'am," he assured her. "I'll be right back."

He returned to his patrol car. Doris trembled, her heart palpitating, and willed herself to conceal her emotions. The officer approached her vehicle and shined his flashlight inside her car.

"I'm not going to give you a ticket this time, but be careful from now on," he warned. "Thank you," she replied.

He took one last look at backseat and noticed the one remaining box, but it didn't look suspicious to him. He said goodbye and drove off. Emma's mother regained her composure and continued her search for the nearest hospital. She followed a nearby sign and pulled up to the exit doors of the hospital. She removed the box, quickly scanned the area, and placed it down on the steps. At the time, she was confident that she had done the best thing for her daughter.

I can't believe I was able to sit through Emma's entire tale. I guess the human mind truly is capable of remembering even the slightest details.

As I had suspected, Doris Blackstone had abandoned those children at the very church and hospital I'd been looking into. Quite the drastic reaction, if you ask me, but I guess things were different back in those days and in that part of the country.

I thank Emma for her time and return back to the motel to pack up my things. I have to get back to New York as soon as I possibly can.

Chapter 42

*T*ime is running out; Michael's scheduled to be executed in just a few days. I still need to find that one piece, really just a scrap, of evidence to indisputably link Michael to his brother Casey. A blood sample would have to be drawn from each of them to see if they match.

I relay my plan to Sweeney and Andrew Fox, and the two of them manage to obtain blood from both Michael and Casey. Optimistic, Andrew also starts the process of securing a stay of execution. The governor is the only person who can grant such a request, so Fox has to find a way to penetrate the bureaucracy. Good thing he's a lawyer. I've always found them to be quite resourceful under the gun.

It turns out that the governor is out of town and can't be reached until the evening of Michael's execution. Andrew frantically pleads his case to the Attorney General's office, but the request goes unanswered.

The governor likely wants to maintain his self-proclaimed tough stance on crime, a key issue in his campaign, and avoid any kind of public controversy. He's always said, and I believe this is a direct quote, "You commit the crime, you do the time, or, in this case, lose your life." He wouldn't go back on his word. It's strictly politics for him; he plans to seek re-election.

The hours are ticking away, and our efforts to save Michael's life are slowly slipping. In one last desperate attempt, Andrew asks Detective Sweeney to interrogate Malloy another time and try to get a confession out of him. But Sweeney's out of the office, likely on a case that's actually within his jurisdiction.

Andrew leaves an urgent message, requesting to be contacted immediately upon the detective's return to the station. Pacing back and forth in his office, Andrew tries to maintain his composure. Time is his worst enemy. Call after call is transferred to his office, but he declines to respond to anyone except Detective Sweeney.

Finally, his secretary announces that Sweeney's on the line.

"Detective Sweeney, this is Andrew," he answers.

"Yes, I'm damn well aware of that. I called *you*. Now what's all this commotion about? I was out grocery shopping," the detective says. "Er—on a case, I mean."

"I need your help."

"What more can I do, Mr. Fox?"

"I'm running out of time. I need you to get that confession from Malloy."

"That asshole ain't gonna talk any more," Sweeney insists.

"You don't understand. We still haven't heard back from the Governor's office, and Michael is scheduled to die within the next few hours. This is our last chance. Our only chance to save an innocent man's life!"

"Okay, I'll give it another shot," the detective tells him with a grimace.

Sweeney swings by the office and summons Casey Malloy to an interrogation room. Drilling him with pointed accusations, a markedly more aggressive tactic than he had previously employed.

He looks Casey straight in the eyes and warns him, "We got ourselves a pile of evidence stacked up against you. Why don't you stop playing games and tell me the whole tale?"

"I already toldja everything ya asked for. You ain't done half as much for me. What's this new evidence?" asks Casey.

"We searched your room at the boarding house. Turned up a trench coat and a fine pair of women's panties. They were concealed in a hidden compartment. Now ain't that a hoot?"

Casey doesn't flinch.

"Those were some old things that were in the way. That's why I stored 'em there. I was gonna throw them out."

"Women's underwear? What are you doin' with them?"

"They were my old girlfriend's. I kept them as a memento. I loved that girl. My sweet, sweet Jolene."

"Jolene, huh? What was her last name?"

"Timberwalk. Jolene Timberwalk."

"That's funny," Sweeney snorts. "These panties we found have the initials: 'M.S.' inside them. Now why would Jolene Timberwalk write that on her underwear?

"I-I-I-dunno," Casey stammers.

"Ain'that a hoot. So I caught you on that one. Now what about the trench coat?"

"I grew out of it and figured I'd pawn it. I had no other place to keep it till then, so I put it up in the ceiling."

"Casey, you're lying through your teeth," Detective Sweeney snaps. "I want you to listen up real good. We know exactly where these items came from, and you're in deep shit. How's that? We've tied them to a murder up in New York."

"I don't know what you're talking about."

"Someone up there is taking the rap for your dirt, and he's gonna die because of what you've done, Casey. If you have one ounce of compassion left, you can prove it now. How could you do this to your own blood? He's your brother, for Chrissake! Do something right for once! Trust me, you're gonna be tried for this case either way."

Casey processes that last bit, then nods his head in resignation.

"I knew you'd come to your senses," Sweeney says.

Detective Sweeney checks his watch, knowing that precious time had elapsed. If he's to save Michael's life, he has to get a confession rather quickly.

"I'm going to record this conversation as well." He turns on his recorder.

"What's your name?"

"Casey, Casey Malloy."

"Do I have your permission to record this interview?"

"Yeah," Casey replies.

"Go ahead. Tell me about New York."

Casey spills the beans. And I mean all of the beans.

"It was back in the late sixties. I was walkin' down the avenue on my way to the restaurant where I worked as a dishwasher. Passing a newspaper stand, I noticed a headline on the front page of the Wall Street Journal. I glanced at it for a second, and the picture on the front page caught my attention. The guy looked just like me! I bought the newspaper and stashed it in my backpack since I was already runnin' late. I was fixin' to read the article during my lunch hour.

When the time came for my break, I started readin' the story. Who was this—whaddya call it—doppelganger of mine who got all successful an' stuff on Wall Street. Something came over me; I was flippin' mad, overcome with jealously an' such. I wanted to be in his shoes. I was tired'a leadin' a life that goin' nowhere. Right then and there, I made up my mind to do somethin' about it. That night, I packed my suitcase and took all the money I'd saved up. I stashed my luggage in the local bus terminal that mornin' on the way to work. I was gonna rob the restaurant's cash register.

I had myself a routine for closing up the place; I'd clean up and empty the trashcans, includin' the one sitting right beneath under the register. When nobody was lookin', I made my move, stickin' my hand in the register and helpin' myself to whatever I could grab. I left and ran straight for the bus terminal, where I purchased a ticket to New York City without being detected.

After getting to the Big Apple, I checked into a fleabag motel off Broadway, and I planned my next move. I cleaned up my scruff to make sure I looked exactly like that Aronstein chump.

I started by obtaining temporary employment in the area near where I was stayin' at. Once I got my routine down, workin' menial jobs each day, I started takin' a subway to the financial district on my days off.

From the article, I'd learnt where he made his bread. I stalked Michael when he left his office, wearin' shades to disguise my identity. I even got myself a wig from a local shop. I watched every move the prick made, and I followed the asshole to the finest restaurants and some of the most fanciest men's stores in Manhattan. I went as far as to stand right next to him at one of those stores. The blunderin' idiot didn't even recognize me, his twin brother.

There was one particular restaurant that he was frequentin'. I noticed that he always left with a cute cocktail waitress. One rainy night, I stood outside and followed him as he caught a cab from his office to this lounge. He walked into the place, but before I knew it, he was out the door and hailin' a cab. This time, he came out without the pretty waitress at his side. I hailed another cab and had him followed 'til he reached his destination. I saw him exit the cab at Madison Avenue in Midtown, and I did the same.

It was raining cats and dogs that night, that's fer damn sure. I watched him cross the street and head into an apartment building. Michael was wearin' a tan trench coat and carryin' an umbrella by his side. Watchin' from a distance, I scanned the windows on each floor to see if I could get some sorta idea as to what apartment he was enterin'. Then I saw Michael and this familiar cocktail waitress standin' at one of the corner apartment windows. I counted to the eleventh floor.

I waited for a while in the pourin' rain. I saw Michael leave the building and wave down another cab. As he left, I spotted that he didn't have his umbrella at his side. With a surefire excuse to get up into that cute waitress's apartment, I easily fooled the doorman at the front desk. I looked just like the guy and wore the same trench coat, which I'd nicked from a local department store.

I took the elevator up to the eleventh floor and found the slut's apartment. I knocked on the door and saw her eye peep through hole in the door. Thinkin' that I was Aronstein, she let me in. I told her that I forgot my umbrella.

Right when I entered, she lunged at me and tried to kiss me, hopin' to reconcile after some sort of an argument. I picked her up and carried her into to her bedroom, tossed her in bed and climbed up on top of her.

We kissed for a moment, and then I started to take off her clothes. She reciprocated by removing my trench coat. But my sleeveless T exposed a tattoo of my old girlfriend's name on my right tricep. She realized that I wasn't Michael and began to scream and resist.

243

She kicked me in the chest with all of her strength and knocked me into the wooden dresser. But she didn't have nowhere to go. I grabbed a pillow and held it out in front of me to block her blows. I managed to get in close enough to pin her down on the floor by her shoulders, smother her with the pillow until she went limp. At that point, there was no reason not to have sex with her. Her body was still warm.

I got dressed, ransacked the bureau, and took a pair of panties as a souvenir. I also snatched any jewelry and cash I could get my hands on. Then I took a subway home. That's what happened. Detective. Everything there is to know. Now lemme get outta here. I ain't feelin' so hot."

"One last question," Sweeney started, "I gotta know—"

"What's that?"

"How'd ya think that would change your life? Why follow Michael?"

"I was gonna pickpocket him, go to the bank, pose as this Aronstein guy. Withdraw all his funds. Rob his home. Figured there'd be a lot of expensive jewelry lyin' around."

"Not the worst plan I've ever heard. That's enough for now."

Sweeney rings Andrew back. "We have a confession. I have it all on tape."

Chapter 43

*I*t had been a long and winding road for both Michael and Andrew. Andrew did everything in his power to prevent this day from happening. He filed countless appeals on Michael's behalf, but his efforts were in vain. This is the last and final straw. The case is too far-gone to stay the execution.

Andrew's back is up against the wall. With only twenty minutes left before the execution, they have to reach the governor some way, somehow. In a last desperate attempt, Andrew contacts the Attorney General and tells him about the new evidence. Apparently convinced, he contacts the Governor's mansion. In a rare stroke of good fortune, the governor had just arrived from a political function and is able to respond to the call.

After Andrew relays all of the circumstances of the case, the governor requests to hear the actual confession for himself before making a decision. They call Detective Sweeney, who plays the tape for the governor. With new compelling evidence and only minutes left, the governor calls the warden at the prison to stay the execution. A prison guard answers the phone and transfers the call to the execution chambers. But the guard assigned to the phones isn't at his desk; he'd needed to take a bathroom break before the execution got underway.

One ring…

Two rings…
Three rings…
Four rings….
Five…..

"Pick up the phone, dammit," he thinks to himself.

Still no answer. The Governor bites his lip, anxious to relay the urgent message. He slams the phone down and exhales deeply. He looks down at his watch. There are only a few minutes left. Then he tries calling again.

One ring…
Two rings…
Three ri—

The guard finally picks up. He waves his arm to get the Warden's attention. McCluskey steps outside the chambers to answer the call.

"This is the Governor. Stop the execution!"

"What? I didn't hear you clearly," McCluskey responds.

The governor repeats, even louder, "Stop the execution, dammit!"

With seconds to go, the warden hangs up the phone and locks his eyes on Michael through the large glass window. McCluskey then motions to the guards inside the chamber to stop the execution. A blinking red light appears on the switchboard just as the guard prepares to pull the switch. He doesn't see McCluskey violently waving his arms. The guard's hand inches closer and closer to the handle. Suddenly, Warden McCluskey bursts through the door, screaming at the top of his lungs, "Stop the execution! I repeat! Stop the execution!" Startled, the guard leaps backwards from the switch and nearly trips over himself trying to avoid the lunging Warden.

With that order, Michael's life is spared.

Michael awakens in a state of confusion. He's led back to his prison cell, still unaware that he'll never have to walk that path again.

Applause and jubilation resonates from the protestors outside the prison walls. Michael's prayers were finally answered. He's getting the second chance in life that he so desperately sought.

The dark cloud hovering over his head has suddenly lifted. His tainted reputation as a calculated killer would be nullified. His ruined life seems to have a new glimmer of hope and he can now start to pick up the crumbled pieces.

The sun is finally back to shining in Michael's corner.

Chapter 44

*A*fter the new evidence came to light, the case of "The People of New York vs. Michael Aronstein" was reopened. Michael was exonerated of all charges and became a free man. He did eventually meet up with his brother, in the strangest of circumstances.

The day he was released from prison, a van brought a group of prisoners back from the courthouse. As Michael exited the gate to freedom, he noticed a handful of cuffed and shackled prisoners being escorted back into the facility. Turning his head in curiosity, Michael's eyes met Casey's for the very first time. They stared at each other for a moment, each thinking about what could have been.

Michael tried to pick up the pieces. Precious years had passed him by, and he couldn't wait to reunite with his children and family. But there was still one piece of unsettled business that Michael had to tackle. He needed to make peace with Lauren.

Shortly after his release, he contacted her to make arrangements to see her. She reluctantly accepted, agreeing to meet at a park bench overlooking the East River, where they had shared many quiet moments together.

Michael, sitting on the bench by himself, waited patiently for Lauren to arrive. He looked at his watch. A half hour had passed, and there was still no sign of Lauren. He figured that she had changed her mind and would never agree to see him again.

But as he turned to leave, a voice suddenly echoed, "Hello, stranger," and there appeared Lauren, sitting in a wheelchair. She was afflicted with a form of Multiple Sclerosis. He was startled. He hadn't spoken to or seen her since the day she walked out on him at the police station.

"What happened to you?" he asked.

"It's a long story, and I don't want to get into it right now." Not wanting to upset her, he didn't pry. He only wanted her to feel comfortable.

She had matured but still maintained her beautiful blonde silky hair, blue eyes, and glowing smile that had captured him the first time he laid eyes on her. He still felt that tingling sensation inside, but he recognized that things had changed. They would never be the same.

They sat on the park bench, watching boats pass them by as the sounds of chirping birds, children playing, and the splashes of rushing water filled the air.

Looking into Lauren's eyes, Michael said, "You haven't changed. You're still as beautiful as ever." She smiled her illuminated smile, and tears began to stream from her face.

"Why did you do this, Michael? Couldn't you leave things just well enough alone? Haven't you done enough damage to this family?"

"I couldn't go on living with myself until I told you my side of the story. I know that what I did was wrong, and nothing in this world can ever make it right. But there were underlying factors that caused me to behave as I did. I thought about this a lot while I was in prison.

Having been adopted, I always felt a void in my life. I had always resisted the urge to find out who I really was, and what I was made of. I knew that my parents loved me dearly, but there was some undetectable thing that was missing. As stupid as it sounds, I was angry that I'd never met my birth parents. I never understood why they just abandoned me. I felt cheated, so I acted out and rebelled against some of the most important people in my life. I just couldn't seem to find happiness, even though it was sitting right in my backyard the whole time."

Tears filled his eyes.

"I am so sorry for what I did to you and the children. I can never forgive myself, nor am I asking for your forgiveness. No matter what happens, I will always love you for who you are and admire how well you raised our children."

Still crying, she replied, "I hated you for what you did. I resented everything you stood for. In my mind, you were as good as buried. I mourned your death long before your execution came. I even concealed your letter from the children."

She softened for a moment, and pulled a sheet of paper from her handbag.

"But I brought it with me today. I thought I'd read it before I give it to the kids. Is that okay?"

Michael nodded his head, and she read aloud:

My Dearest Julia, Abbey and Brittney,

By the time you receive this letter, I will be in another place, always watching over all of you. I know that I have caused our family a great deal of hardship, but I never wanted it to turn out this way. I want you to know that your father was not a murderer. I never committed the crime for which I am being punished. I was guilty of having an extramarital affair, but that was the extent of my wrongdoing. I only wish that I could right those wrongs.

In spite of all that has happened to me, the only person I can blame is myself. I am not seeking your forgiveness but merely asking that you remember me for all of my good qualities. Your images pass through my mind every day, and I will never stop thinking of you. I love you all so very much. Please always live in peace and harmony. Watch over your dear mother, who never deserved this disastrous fate. You will all be in my heart for eternity.

I love you always,
Dad

After she read the letter, Lauren found room in her heart to forgive her former knight in shining armor. They kissed, their lips trembling as they did on their first date at the drive-in movie theater.

Covering this story has certainly been intriguing. It captivated my interest like none other has in my twenty-five years as a reporter, and I will never forget it.

Michael finally met his biological mother in Alabama. He discovered that Billy's love and devotion to Emma never wavered. One month after Emma delivered, she and Billy ran away and eloped in August of 1933. On their honeymoon, they were in a horrific automobile accident. A truck ran a stop sign and broadsided them.

Billy died at the scene, but Emma survived. It happened on the same day as Michael's bris.

Casey Malloy was tried for the murder of Maria Salvatez, as well as other unsolved rape cases. He was convicted and received a life sentence without parole. His public defender pleaded insanity and gained the jury's sympathy.

The state of New York was ordered to pay restitution to Michael for all of his years of pain and suffering.

Well, it's getting rather late now and it's time for me to shut off the lights in my office. As usual, I'm the last one out, so I figure I'll stop at O'Malley's to get a beer before I head home and get some rest before starting my new assignment tomorrow.